Olivia's Fall

LOVE AND VAMPIRES
BOOK ONE

RHIANNON FUTCH

*To the dear friends that
keep telling me I got this.
Thank you.
You know who you are.*

Olivia

Nims is bouncing with eagerness for our evening walk. It is the last walk of the day for us and our favorite. We go out right as it is getting dark and meander through the park down the road. She gets to sniff all the things that have been through the area and I get to trail after her.

Her short, dark coat of fur makes her hard to see in the evening, which has made her presence a surprise to some men that wanted to bother me. But those interruptions to our walk have been few. Mostly we just enjoy the night walk and being together. My Nims has been my best friend since the day I got her three years ago. My parents were horrified when they saw her. They said her sweet hound face looked like a demon and I needed to get rid of her. I told them no, flat out.

They found every reason to say I should get rid of her. From the demon eyes to the black coat, they just knew

Nims was evil. I knew differently, and I kept her. I am so glad I did.

Tonight the moon is just a sliver and I have to step carefully as Nims leads me through the park. The air is still warm from the heat of the day but smells of the coolness of night. She has finished her business and we are on our way home when I hear someone shout, "Hey bitch! Don't you hear us talking to you?"

The woman talking is walking toward me with some of her friends. I look around to see if there is anyone else around, but it's just Nims and me. Nims is growling low in her throat as I ask, "Are you talking to me?"

The group of women striding toward me looks mean in the dim light of the park. One of them says, "Bitch, yes, we are talking to you! You fuckin' know we are Stephanie!"

"Stephanie? My name is Olivia. I think you have the wrong person." I start to back away as the group gets closer. Tugging the leash so Nims steps back with me.

The one at the front of the group says, "Now you're just making me mad, Stephanie. I ain't got no wrong person. I know you are the one that has been messing around with my man. And tonight was the last time you got to see him."

I want to run, but I don't think I can outrun them. My heart is pounding in my chest as I say, "I promise it wasn't me. I don't know you or your man. I wouldn't do that. And my name is Olivia, not Stephanie. You've got the wrong girl!"

The women are spreading out around us, I don't know what to do. How am I going to protect Nims when I don't think I can protect myself? The leader of the group gets right in my face, saying, "You gonna learn tonight, bitch! We don't tolerate stupid, man-stealing bitches around here!"

The first punch comes out of nowhere. It knocks me back into one of the other women. Everything is a blur from there until they leave us laying on the ground, spitting on me as they walk away. I can hardly move, everything hurts so much. I hear Nims whimper and I look toward the sound. She seems as bad off as I am. I don't think we are going to live through this. I can feel the life leeching out of me. My Nims is just a few feet away. If I am going to die tonight, I am going to be by her side.

Moving my arms hurts, but I drag myself over to her. She lifts her big head and lays it on my chest as I curl up around her. My eyelids are so heavy, closing as I use the last of my strength to put my arm around her.

Callum

The party I am steadily walking toward isn't even the last place I want to be tonight. Being the ambassador for our family sucks. I could be at home with someone warm and willing. Or reading. Or doing damn near anything but going to this stupid party with a bunch of stuck up vampires that want me around for the clout.

The park is really nice tonight at least, but I'll be glad to go home. I will conclude the business I am handling for the family tonight. If everything goes according to plan. One contract to sign at this party and tomorrow I can go home.

A deep hunger hits me out of nowhere, causing me to

stop where I am. I see nothing, but I sniff the air. Oh, that smells good. The scent of blood in the air must have been what caused it. I should continue on to the party but... I think I need to find the source of the blood.

Following the scent, I find a woman curled up around a dog. They are both bleeding. It looks like they were attacked and left to die just off the path. The scent of her blood is divine. Once she is cleaned up and put in something better than cutoffs and a tank top, she looks like she would be a hell of a prize. I love a prize. My mind made up, I unbutton my shirt cuff and roll up the sleeve as I kneel next to her. One slip of a nail down the length of my wrist has it open and dripping the dark, viscous blood of a vampire that hasn't had fresh blood in entirely too long. Stretching my wrist to hover over her mouth, I let the blood do its work. It is only a minute or two before she begins to actively swallow the blood. Some of it is splashing on the dog, but that dog is surely already gone.

Her eyes open, the most hypnotic green eyes I have seen in many years. The blood from my wrist has stopped falling. I didn't pay enough attention to keep it open. She looks so adorably dirty and confused. I offer her my hand, saying, "Come, sit up. You'll feel better soon."

She asks, "Who are you?"

I don't answer as I help her stand. Instead I say, "Do you live nearby?"

She nods, saying, "Yes, but I thought for sure I was dying. What happened?" She turns to look at her dog, "Is my Nims going to be okay?"

Her voice breaks a little. Poor thing. The party should be plenty distracting for her. "I think the dog is done for.

But you are alive and ready to start a whole new life. I have an appointment that I really must keep. So we'll have to do that first. After I finish, though, you will be the perfect reason I need to leave early. We'll get you fed while we are there, though."

Tugging her along as I talk, she is stumbling and keeps looking back at the damn dog. We only get a few steps away when she plants her feet, saying, "No. I won't leave her."

As she tries to yank her hand away, I grip it tighter, saying, "The dog is dead or will be dead soon. You have a whole new life to get to living... sort of. Anyway, we need to go."

I know she is going to cause a scene as soon as her eyes narrow at my hand gripping hers. She snatches her hand out of mine, snarling, "I am not leaving my Nims. That is my best friend and you are just a fucking stranger. Fuck the fuck off, I am taking her home and if she is still alive, to a vet."

Sighing heavily, I say, "Fine. You live nearby, right?"

She nods as she walks back to the dog, saying, "Yes, why?"

"Because you are still new and you are going to need guidance for the next few years. Look, I will come find you later tonight. If you aren't home, then I will be back tomorrow night. Make sure you are inside before the sun comes up," I walk over to grab her chin and make her look at me, "before the sun comes up. Do you understand?"

She glares at me, saying, "If you don't get your hands off of me, I am going to scream my head off. Who do you think you are, anyway?"

Removing my hand from her incredibly soft skin, I say,

"I am your sire. You are going to have a lot of questions and you will understand everything once they get answered. For now, I will leave you to tend your dog while I handle my business. I will see you soon, agreed?"

She stands with the dog in her arms, "Fine, I am guessing then you will explain how I am not dead and don't even really feel injured?"

"Yes, I will. Until then, my little one." I leave her there, using my speed to make up for the time that I spent arguing with her.

* * *

Olivia

The strange man that never told me his name while he was saying all that cryptic shit disappears into the night and I hug my Nims close. I can feel her breathing, shallow as it is. She licks my face and neck as I carry her home. I can't help being grateful for it because it lets me know she is still alive. It takes me little time to make it back to the apartment and I'm not even tired carrying Nims. It must be the adrenaline. Getting her inside, I lay her on my bed. She seems to be breathing a little easier as I pick up my phone from next to the bed and start searching for emergency vets.

An hour later, I just want to cry. Every one of them wants the money right now and I just don't have that kind of cash. Thank God that Nims is still breathing. She looks to be sleeping peacefully. I am so tired. The sun is lighting the sky through the sheer curtains as I lay down next to Nims. "I don't know what to do, Nims. Hopefully, whatever miracle fixed me is working on you. I will be lost without you. Please, please live. I need you."

Nims licks my face a little more and I just let her, even though I usually would not. I am so tired. I feel myself slipping off to sleep even as she slows down with the licking of my face.

O livia

Why is my face so wet? What is that — "Nims! Stop licking me! Ugh!" Pushing her back and wiping my face, I sit up. Everything that happened last night rushes into my mind and I look at Nims, terrified that she is going to fall over or something. She is happily sitting on the edge of the bed, tail thumping as she grins at me.

I reach over to run my hands over her, just to reassure myself that she really is ok. She sits patiently through my checking, leaning her bulk against me in her sort of hug. I swear she knows what I am doing and why.

As I run my hands over her, I realize I am starving. How long were we asleep?

A glance at the window tells me it is still night, so it can't have been that long. Grabbing my phone, I head into the kitchen, telling Nims, "Come on, let's get you and me fed."

Checking the notifications on my phone, I see that I have a voicemail from work. Odd, I am not due in for hours yet. My jaw drops as I listen to the message asking why I am not at work today and who do I think I am not calling them to let them know I wouldn't be coming in. Oh fuck, tell me I didn't sleep for the whole day. The date on my phone is definitely reading as Monday night.

"Nims, we might be screwed. I don't know if they are going to be all right with this. I might lose my job." She whimpers up at me, her tail thumping the floor a couple of times. The people in the apartment under ours hit the ceiling of their apartment. I hear them shouting, "Keep it quiet up there!"

I feel a sharp desire to go down there and do some shouting of my own. Instead, I take a deep breath and try to remember that I want to keep living here. The rent is a price I can afford, and it is close to work. I get some food down for Nims and realize that I am still filthy from last night. I don't even want to see what I look like. A hot shower does have me feeling a little more human. I am still a little shocked at how much blood washed off of me. The mirror is foggy and easy to ignore while I brush my teeth. After that is finished, I really have no choice but to wipe away the moisture on the mirror and have a look at the damage.

Oh my god. There is nothing. How is that even possible? I know we were beaten and left for dead. How is it that there are no marks? Nims is feeling fine, but I thought it was because she is a dog. How is this possible? What the hell is wrong with me? And how am I going to tell my boss that I wasn't at work because I was assaulted when there are no bruises? No evidence of any kind?

Fuck me, I didn't think this could get any worse, but here we are. If I get kicked out of here because I lost my job and can't pay rent, I can't go home. Not unless I give up Nims and that isn't an option. She is more family to me than anyone. Including my parents. I have to figure out something. But first, Nims is probably as dirty as I was. I need to at least take a brush to her. It is near eleven by the time I have finished and Nims is antsy to go outside. I am starving, but I can wait till we get back.

Leashing her up and grabbing the cross body bag I carry to put phone, keys, and poop bags in has us heading out the door. I am more than a little glad it is so late. What if those women were there again tonight? I don't imagine they are going to take it well if I tell them to make sure the beating leaves marks this time so I can get my absence from work excused.

Tonight, Nims is pulling hard on the leash, trying to guide me into the wooded area here. Seeing a group of people in the distance, I decide to let her pull me into the woods. She keeps pulling me till we are well into the woods and then she just stops. Looking at the leash and then at me. Fear shoots through my heart as I realize what she wants. My hands shake as I reach over and unclip her leash. She bumps my cheek with her nose and then takes off running through the woods.

My heart sinks. Sitting there, I wonder, did I just let my best friend run away from me? I want her safe. If she doesn't want to live with me, I would rather find her the right place for her than leave her wandering the woods. The sound of something big being dragged toward me interrupts my dark thoughts. I scoot into the bushes a bit, watching. Then I see Nims. She is dragging something. Standing up, I walk over and she drops the leg of the thing, grinning up at me. It's a deer. Oh my god, it's a deer. As I look at this poor creature in horror, the scent of its blood reaches me. Hunger, so sharp I feel it in my throat, rages through me. I want nothing more than to drink every last drop from this poor deer. Oh god, what is happening to me? Next thing I know, I am on my knees, drinking deeply from its throat.

My hunger eases and I realize what I am doing. Releasing my hold on the deer, I scramble back away from it. What have I done? Nims is sitting next to the creature, watching me. She looks down at the hindquarters of the deer and my eyes drift down, following the line of her gaze. There are four distinct holes, dripping a small amount of blood. "Oh Nims, what happened to us last night? What is wrong with us?"

She walks over to me and seats herself next to me, leaning into me. My arm goes around her like it always does. Looking at this deer, I can't help but wonder what is going to happen to us. I know this isn't normal. It isn't ok. I read about vampires in stories, but that can't be what is happening here. Can it? You have to be bit first, right?

That's what happened in the movies. Oh god, what am I going to do? Nims nudges my shoulder with her nose. When I don't move, she nudges me with some force and I look at her, saying, "Nims, what?" She whimpers and looks toward home. "Oh! Oh! Let me get your leash on. We absolutely do not need people looking closely at us." Fuck, what if I have blood on my face? Pulling my phone out of my bag, I hold the camera icon on the screen till it brings up the app. There isn't a whole lot of light, but I can see well enough to get my face wiped off. Using the light of the phone, I check Nims's face too, and then my shirt. Because there has never been a meal to pass my lips that my shirt didn't also sample. Sure enough, there it is. I can tell there is a little bit of blood on the dark blue shirt. We do not need people seeing this. Oh, I know! Kneeling down in front of Nims I put my hands on her legs and give them the lightest of tugs. She definitely thinks I have a screw loose somewhere as she sits back to let me lift her paws. I take those dirty paws and rub them down the front of my shirt, making sure one of them gets the blood stain. When I finish, it looks like Nims jumped on me. Perfect.

Clipping her leash on her again, I tell her, "Let's go home so I can have my breakdown in the comfort of our place instead of out here where anyone could walk up on us."

We walk fast to get home. I can feel the anxiety eating away at my control and I cannot be sitting somewhere out around anything that could bleed. What if I get hungry again? We make it into the apartment and once Nims is unhooked from her leash, I just sit on the couch. Nims curls up next to me, perfectly content. Whatever happens, I have to make sure I keep her safe. What am I going to do? Maybe I can talk to Candy, Sharon, and Lily? I mean, after Nims, they are my best friends. They would want to help me. We can figure something out between the four of us for sure. I feel a little better with even that much of a plan in place. Grabbing the remote, I turn on the tv and settle in to watch some crappy, late-night programs.

Three

Olivia

It burns. What is burning me? There's nothing here — my eyes fly open and I see the patch of sunlight on my arm, smoke rising from my skin. Snatching my arm out of the sunlight, I just sit there for a moment, stunned. What is wrong with me? Why is the sunlight burning me? Getting up from the couch we fell asleep on last night, I grab my umbrella and use it to push the curtains fully closed. Everyone I know thought this long umbrella was a ridiculous purchase, but I sure am glad for it today. Since I am awake, I decide to message my friends and ask them to come over. I need my friends to help me figure out what the hell is wrong with me.

And more importantly, how to fix it.

They show up two hours later, by which time I have been pacing the floor for an hour and a half. I have to be careful opening the door to them. The sunlight is hitting the front of my apartment at this time of day. Dammit, I am really going to miss sitting in the sun. There is nothing quite like a chilly fall day sitting in a patch of sunlight. The three of them wander in. I can smell the delicious aroma of the coffees they carry. I hope one of them is for me. Cindy is talking about her latest boyfriend drama as they seat themselves on my couch. I sit down in the chair and Nims comes to sit next to me. It is then that Sharon looks over at me and says, "Olivia! You had work done! Your mom is going to be so pissed!"

"What are you talking about? I didn't have any work done. You saw me last week. That is not enough time to heal from having had work done. And where do you think I would have gotten the money for that? You know I can barely afford this apartment."

Cindy looks around my space, a small frown on her lips, "I confess, I've never really understood why you insisted on having this space. You could have just kept living with your parents, the same as we did with ours. Why did you move in here?"

Gritting my teeth, I answer the same question she has asked every time she came over here. "I needed my own space, is all. My parents are a little overbearing, and I wanted some space outside of them."

And to be able to have my privacy, but that isn't something we can talk about. Pamela nods, "Yes, and you wanted to get that awful dog of yours. I think your parents had some sort of issue with the dog. It was poorly behaved or something?"

I watch as Cindy and Sharon nod like that was what happened when they know what really happened. "Pam, why are you lying? It doesn't make you better if you change the facts, it makes you a sinner. Good thing we aren't

Catholics. You would be saying a lot of Hail Marys and Our Fathers after your next confession."

Pam narrows her eyes, saying, "It wasn't a lie." She lifts her round chin, saying, "They told me that when I went to visit them. Which you would know about if you visited them more often."

My eyes roll of their own accord. "Yes, Pam, I know well that you visit my parents and that you try to get them to talk shit about me. They tell me how weird it is every time you show up on their doorstep. They said they would quit answering the door, but you go to the same church and they just feel sorry for anyone reduced to visiting someone's parents to try to speak poorly about them." Shaking my head, I tell them, "This isn't what I called you here for. I called you here because I need help."

Cindy and Sharon lean forward, and Pam turns toward me again. I tell them the entire story, from being attacked to the part about the deer. The part about Nims may have been omitted for her safety. I just had a feeling it wouldn't be a good idea. Their mouths are hanging open by the time I finish my story.

Pam is the one that stands, saying, "You're possessed. Cindy, Sharon, we need to go before she brings in another demon to possess us."

Cindy gasps, standing as she says, "Is that possible?" She looks at me, saying, "You wouldn't do that to us, would you, Olivia?"

Sharon stands and grabs Cindy's arm, tugging her toward the door Pam is already headed for, saying, "We are not sitting in here alone with a demon to find out. We need to go!"

Tears are running unchecked down my face as I plead with them, "Don't go, I swear I'm not possessed! You are supposed to be my friends. Oh God, help me. I don't know what to do."

Pam smiles a triumphant little smile as she urges the other two out the door. Nims growls at her and she loses all the color in her face as she runs out. Hugging Nims, I tell her, "Thank you. I should have known better than to call them. But they are the only human friends I have and I don't know what to do. I can't go in to work tomorrow. I'll die trying to get there. What are we going to do, Nims?"

* * *

Monday has come so quickly. I managed to wake up this morning, but it was a struggle. Taking a deep breath, I call my boss. She picks up on the first ring, saying, "Where were you Friday? We didn't make quota because you weren't here. You better have a real good reason I shouldn't fire you right now."

Shit. "I'm sorry Tina, I would have been there if I could. You know I want the hours. A group of women attacked me Thursday night. They left me for dead in the park. I am actually calling to ask if I can work from home. I look terrible and would be a distraction at the office."

Tina sighs, saying, "You are going to need to provide a doctor's note to work from home."

"But you had me start bringing my computer home so I could work from home. This is the perfect time for that."

"You bringing home the computer is for our convenience, not yours. Your job is still on the line. If you can't produce a doctor's note, you are going to be fired. In any case, you are not returning to work until you have that note. That includes at home work. I expect that note on my desk by the end of the day." *Click*

I stare at my phone for a moment. She really hung up on me. This isn't good. If my so-called friends think I had work done, the chances of me convincing anyone else that I was beaten and left for dead are exactly zero.

Grabbing the laptop in front of me, I open it and pull up an online job listing service. Even as I start to type in the search bar, my phone starts ringing. I look at it and see my boss is calling me. My heart freezes in my chest as I realize what computer I am using. This is not my personal computer. Hitting the button as I bring the phone to my ear, I answer, saying, "Hi Tina, did you change your mind about letting me work from home?"

Tina snarls at me, "No! You are fired! Every one of our computers lets us know what happens on them. How dare you job search on our computer! You better have that computer up here before you come to pickup your last paycheck. I can't believe you would stop being a team player simply because we require a doctor's note. How could you, Olivia?"

The answer is in my mouth; the words aching to be set free. Instead, I hang up the phone. I'm not an employee, I don't have to talk to them. Before they can send any signals to the computer I unplug the internet and factory reset the thing. My time working at that rent-to-own store is paying off today. Setting that laptop on the coffee table, I stand to go get my laptop. I am mid-stretch when someone knocks with vigor on my door. The curtains are completely closed and I am incredibly grateful for that right now. I look at Nims and put a finger to my lips, and she nods. How could I not love that dog? I pad quietly over to the door and peek out the peephole. It is Preacher Kramer standing out there, a large bag in his right hand and that ridiculous giant cross he keeps on him strapped to his left hip. Of all the people I am not letting be in my home alone with me and Nims, this guy tops the list. Backing away from the door, I go sit next to Nims and we both watch the door till we hear him walk away. I breathe a sigh of relief as his footsteps fade away. Getting back up, I go fetch my laptop from my bedroom and return to find Nims sniffing at a note on my floor just in front of the door.

Dread fills my heart as I walk over and pick it up. Flipping open the folded page, I find a note from the apartment manager that says I have one week to find a job or I am getting evicted. That bitch Tina must have called him. My eyes are filling with tears. What am I going to do?

Four

Olivia

I don't understand any of it. It doesn't matter how much I eat. The hunger never goes away. Except for that one time, that I took Nims out and she brought back a deer. But that presents its own problem. Why do I need to drink blood to feel full? Just as my pity party is climbing to tears, I hear a knock at my door. Nims growls quietly and I know my parents must be out there. Checking the peephole, I see them standing out there, just as expected. Mother with her blond hair curled and sprayed into place so well that I can smell the Aquanet from here. My father, lanky and slightly stooped, standing next to her with his dishwater hair parted to one side the way it has been his entire life. With a sigh, I open the door for them. As soon as the door opens, a paper gets shoved at me. My apartment manager is standing off the side of my parents, saying, "You are hereby served with your eviction notice. We will change the locks on the day you are to be out. We don't tolerate demons here."

My jaw drops. What the hell? Who? I shout at his back as he walks away, "I am not a demon! This is not legal!"

He shrugs but never slows his stride. My parents walk past me into my apartment and too late, I see that Preacher Kramer is with them. Fucking wonderful.

My mother asks, "Can you put away that dreadful dog? I feel certain that she is the cause of this entire mess." Nims narrows her eyes and her jowls tighten. I swear that dog understands every word we say. Taking a seat in the chair next to Nims, I put a hand on her head and say, "I will not. This home is as much Nims as it is mine. If you don't want to see her, don't feel comfortable around her, don't come here. I come to visit you regularly. And why did you bring him?" I jerk a thumb toward the priest, still standing near the door like he thinks he is blocking the exit. Moron. The burning sun is blocking me from leaving, not you.

My mother looks at my father and he says, "Well, your friends came by and told us about their visit. About how different you look and how you were telling them wild stories. They also told us you might be possessed. Has something happened to you recently?"

Fucking Pam. I know this is her fault. I bet the bitch stopped to talk to the manager too. "They heavily exaggerated the details. And honestly, do I look possessed?"

Father frowns and mother studies me intently before saying, "Not exactly. You look like someone that sold her soul for unearthly beauty. What did you do?"

Preacher Kramer clears his throat, "Occasionally demonic possession will present as a temporary enhancement of the features. That is part of how they entice the weak willed among us that haven't fully accepted Christ into their hearts."

I look at Nims, and she rolls her eyes. I fully agree with her. He is reaching, hard. My mother and father are completely taken in. Father says, "We really want you to consider allowing Preacher Kramer to perform an exorcism on you." Mother nods firmly, her self righteous glare firmly in place.

Rage courses through me at the very idea. I remember what he did to my friend. The only real friend I had. Three days of tormenting a ten-year-old that they decided was possessed. It was brutal. They showed us videos as a cautionary tale. To ensure that we would all accept Christ into our hearts and never stray from the church's teachings. It terrified me then and now the idea that my parents would try to convince me to allow that to happen to me, no. My hunger grows sharp suddenly and I am a little frightened that if they don't leave soon, they are going to be certain that there is a demon inside me. I realize that I have been holding my breath, and I exhale. Taking a breath in, I say, "Maybe you don't remember what he did to Kelly, but I do. He will not be performing anything on me, ever."

My mother's lips thin till there is nothing left. I wonder again how it is possible that I came from these people. She says, "If you will not allow the exorcism, you are no longer welcome at our home. We will disown you. We cannot have a daughter of ours parading around town, possessed for all the world to see."

I feel tears burning at the backs of my eyes. Nims presses her shoulder against my knee. Looking at her and the love shining from her eyes, it gives me courage. "I am wearing a cross. I couldn't wear a cross if I am possessed, right?"

My parents look at Preacher Kramer, who shakes his head and says, "That is an old trick that demons use. They create an illusion of a cross. If we were to dip that cross in holy water, we would find the mark of the devil."

The tears that threatened before are flowing now as I say, "How could you take his word over mine? You know about the things he has done. You know!"

My mother waves her manicured hands in my direction, saying, "You were always so dramatic. I see that having a demon hiding within you has only emphasized the trait. Preacher Kramer has had some... misunderstandings in his youth. But he is not to blame for what he did not know. He isn't accountable to someone demon possessed, anyway. If only you would let him pull that demon from you—"

"It isn't a misunderstanding when people die for the things he does! What do you mean, in his past? He is still doing these things! He is not, under any circumstances, performing anything on me!"

My father's face falls and my mother's lips disappear completely as she says, "Then we will have no daughter until you allow the exorcism to be performed. You will have no help from us. You are disowned and will have no family."

This is more than I can take and I stand, telling them, "I need you all to leave right now." My mother starts to say something else and I shout, "Get out of my house right this instant! Out! Out! Out!"

Frowning at me, they stand and walk to the door. Preacher Kramer hasn't moved. He stares at me as he pulls a card out of his pocket, saying, "Call me when you are ready to be rid of the demon within you."

Pointing at the door, I say, "Get out!" He takes two steps toward the open door and tries to turn back. I am right behind him, so I give him a shove out the door and slam it behind him. I am so grateful that the sun is not beating on my door now. Starting to burn and smoke as I shove a preacher out the door of my apartment will convince no one that I am not, in fact, demonic. Leaning my back against the door, I slide down it to sit on the floor. Nims presses up against me and I put my arms around her. Pressing my face into her fur, I say, "What are we going to do?"

Five

Olivia - ten years later

When the plague that is COVID hit, I thought for sure that I would never leave the house again for anything but walking dogs. I thought I was dreaming the night Nims and I found the Witches Market. Right in the middle of Inverness and not a single human has any idea. Hell, I had no idea until the shutdown had me wandering the streets at night that the Witches Market existed and I am one of the others that can see it. Admittedly, I don't try to make friends. I have my Nims and my rescues, that is enough.

It took me years just to stop running from the church. When I left my apartment, after my entire life came crashing down like the proverbial fallen tower, I thought I would just be homeless for a time. Then Nims and I were attacked one day while we were sleeping. Nims nudges my leg and I realize I am reminiscing when I should be taking her out for her evening walk.

Standing from the desk I have been sitting at since early

this afternoon, I stretch. It isn't really necessary for the vampire that I am, but it still feels nice. I tell the rescues to behave while we are gone and Nims adds her growl to seal the deal. We head out the front door. Night has fallen, and the sky is clear. The air feels crisp and invigorating. Nims is trotting briskly, too briskly for a normal dog. I say, "Nims, honey, slow down." She looks around at the very empty streets and back at me. Laughing, I say, "Fine, let's get there fast." We run toward the town center, moving so fast the humans will never see us. She loves going here. The witches are always o very nice to her, as are the shifter packs. The vampires are pretty indifferent to her, and to me. This suits me even better than how nice the others are. The ones that are nice to us, they make me want to like them. Have me dreaming of having friends and family again.

I am much better off alone than opening myself up to the hurt they could cause if I let them in. I don't know that I could take my life burning to dust like that again. As soon as we step into the Witches Market, we stop. The place is made of magic and to be here is to enter a whole other world. Little twinkle lights are everywhere. I used to call them fairy lights the way most humans do. Then someone was kind enough to tell me the Fae don't exactly like that word, so I make it a point to not use it. The first place we go is the actual store the witches have here in the market. It is a fantastical sort of place.

I pick up a basket on my way in. I remember the first time Nims and I came here was such a scene. The baskets are enchanted. Anything set in them will fly out and make a stack up at the counter. The items from any one basket all congregate in one spot. When the person with that basket arrives at the counter to pay, the items appear next to them, bagged up. However, there isn't a sign announcing that is how things happen. So the first time it happened to us, Nims took off after the item, barking like mad at the thing. I think it was a loaf of bread. The witches thought it was the cutest thing, and she has been a favorite of theirs ever since. They explained to her what was happening just the way I would have, if I had known.

While I don't want to get close to them, I have a great respect for their love of dogs. They wave at me as we pass by the counter. I wave back and Nims gives a little bark that startles the Fae at the counter. When they glare at Nims, she puts her head down and looks away. I smile and shrug at them. The witches already warned me about apologizing to them or thanking them. We won't be doing that. It takes me very little time to shop, since I mostly eat food for the enjoyment of it now. When we get to the counter, Ailsa is there waiting for us. She isn't the one handling the purchase, but I don't really have to pay attention anyway. The witches here are trustworthy. Ailsa comes around the counter and greets Nims first, saying, "Hello, brave warrior woman. How are you today?" Nims butts Ailsa's hand with her head, giving a little whine. Ailsa laughs as she gives her a good scratch behind the ears. Then she turns to me and folds me into a hug. I won't tell her, but I love the hugs. If I ever have to leave here, I will miss them. And that is exactly why I can't be letting these people in any farther than they already are. She releases me and grasps my shoulders, studying my face. I wonder what she is seeing when she says, "The tower came up in a reading for you today. Things are going to change for you. The shell you use to keep everyone out is going to have to go. And the devil card was there. Who is after you child?"

"After me? No-," I stop before I can finish the sentence as I remember the feeling of eyes on me, the man dressed in black with a white spot at the throat that always seems to be around these days. No. I am just imagining things. Shaking my head no, I say, "No one. No one is after me."

Ailsa narrows her eyes, saying, "And what interrupted your thought just then? It wasn't a lovely kitten for Nims to cuddle, now was it?"

With a sigh, I realize she is not letting this go. I may as well confess and I do, saying, "Just some guy hanging around. He hasn't done anything. But he seems to be always around, always watching. I don't know who he is. And sometimes, even when he doesn't seem to be around, I feel eyes watching me. Nims doesn't like him, and I think she feels the eyes too. Do you Nims?"

Nims has been watching and listening intently, and she nods her gigantic head in the affirmative. Ailsa says, "You should always trust your senses. They won't steer you wrong the way heart and mind will. Better yet, trust Nims senses. She isn't bound by silly human sensibilities, the way newer vampires tend to be."

"I will. But now, I really need to get the dog food from the shifter shops. You know how Nims has her favorites. The other dogs like it too."

Ailsa eyes me. My attempt at escape from this wildly uncomfortable conversation is less subtle than I hoped, but she nods, saying, "It's fine. I know you aren't comfortable being cared for by anyone except your Nims. Go on with you, run away to the shifters that will only lust after you and not press you to share your inner world with them."

My cheeks would have been on fire if I were still human. Thankfully, I am not and they are blessedly cool to the touch as I say, "Thank you. I'll be having them bring it over here to be sent home with the rest. That service is the best. I wish you would let me pay for it."

She laughs, telling me, "I know you do. But our output for the synthetic stuff has more than doubled since you started your little business venture. Go, off with you."

Nodding my head at her, I head for the door. This market is a wealth of wonders for someone new to this world like I am. The shop next to this is shoes, but I have never seen shoes like these. The feet they fit often bear more resemblance to Nims feet than mine. Oddly, I never see anyone with feet shaped differently, though I have seen many catch sight of the shoes and dip into the shop. The shifter's pet food shop is just ahead, my musings on footwear having carried me past other shops. This is why even after five years here, I am still looking around like everything is brand new.

Just inside the shop, I have to pause. The shop is a little bit of chaos on any given day and everything gets moved around. Giant bins with compartments full of treats, each type shaped to represent the flavor. Beef treats look like cows, chicken treats look like little chickens. There are a few shapes I am curious about, but not brave enough to ask what they are, as at least one type looks rather human shaped. Today, the area in front of the door is relatively clear.

As Nims and I walk toward what I think is the dog

treats, Blair walks over, saying, "Olivia, so good to see you!" Before I can say anything he envelopes me in a hug, his bulk seeming to surround me in warmth and safety. I don't understand how someone with all these muscles can feel so cuddly, but every time he does this, I just want to curl up with him.

"Blair, you've got to stop hugging me like this if we aren't going to have a nap," I say as I push on the bulk of him.

He laughs as he releases me, but grasps my arm and steers me a different way, saying, "You don't want that section. The treats for your pups and Nims are over here. How is the stray from last week? Is he getting on well with the other dogs?"

"He didn't want to at first. He thought he was going to give me a bite when my back was turned, but Nims told him off. But he's been a gentleman ever since."

Blair laughs again, saying, "Good job, Nims! You take care of our girl, don't let anyone harm her. Even a silly mutt that doesn't know what's good for him. Olivia, how many dogs have you got right now?"

His arm has slipped around my shoulders as he guides me around various bins toward the large one in the corner, saying, "Only fifteen at the moment. I couldn't do this if it weren't for my sweet Nims," I say as I reach over and scratch behind one of her ears. "Her presence and how she tells them off makes all the difference."

He nods, "I imagine it does. A week of food for them like usual?"

"Yes, and," I look at where Nims is snagging a treat from the bin, saying, "it looks like we'll have the rabbit treats this week. Don't forget to charge for the two she ate."

"I'll do no such thing. Nims gets to sample the merchandise." His arm comes away from my shoulders and he takes my hand, saying, "Won't you come to dinner with me? We could have a lovely night, and perhaps a fantastic day. Say you will?"

"Blair, you ask me every time I come in. Don't you tire of the rejection?"

He grins, saying, "Never. I'll ask you until you tell me to stop."

Shaking my head, I tell him, "You are too nice for someone like me. You'd break my heart and there's barely any left to break."

Six

H e nods, serious now, saying, "I wouldn't break your heart, little love. If you would let me in, I just might fix it."

"I don't remember the fairy tales going quite like that. The wolf wasn't trying to fix broken hearts."

He laughs, saying, "Fairy tales aren't really accurate, but we could start with me eating you. See if I can make you scream my name."

And there's the gratitude that I can't blush showing up again. Yet, somehow I suddenly feel quite warm. I fan myself a bit, saying, "Blair, you certainly are persuasive. But, are shifters and vampires supposed to be together? I thought the two breeds preferred to stay separate? Or did I misunderstand?"

He nods, saying, "It was that way once. But now, only the assholes cling to that." He looks away for a moment. Turning back to me, he says, "Some of the vampires down the street still prefer it that way, which is where I presume you heard that?"

He is looking down at me with one brow raised. His lips are pressed together and there is a light in his eyes that suggests he might do violent things to someone based on my answer. Swallowing, I say, "Yes, one of them might have impressed upon me that I should not be seen dating any shifters. I thought maybe that it was just how things were. Humans are shitty like that. I guess I just wasn't really surprised that it would be that way here, too."

He says, "Only the bigoted assholes believe that. And if the rest of the vampires heard him talking to you like that, they would fix his head for him. So, now that you haven't that to worry about, what do you say?"

I really want to. It's been a very long time since I dated anyone and he is so kind, Nims adores him. I look up. His face causes things to stir and flutter in places that haven't been touched in so long. Taking a breath in, I ask him, "Are you sure? I haven't been out with anyone in so long. I don't think I know how anymore."

A deep rumble sounds in his chest and the sound causes pleasant tingles up my spine. He says, "I'll teach you. Tomorrow night?"

His hands are warm on my arms, and he is so tempting. How can I say no when my batteries are dead at home? I tell him, "Yes, yes. Come to the house tomorrow and I'll let you take me out on a date."

His smile is near blinding just before he snatches me up in a bear—er, wolf hug? When he sets me down, he is still smiling that big smile as he says, "Go finish your errands. I'll send the treats and the food over to the witches. Don't worry, I know how much to send over. I'll see you tomorrow." He touches my cheek, so lightly, but it feels so nice that I lean into it a little as my eyes drift closed and he asks, "How long has it been since someone touched you, little love?"

His large hand is cupping my face as I say, "Since before I became a vampire. Ten years."

He sighs, "Little love, that is so long to go without a touch of any kind. Why?"

Opening my eyes, I pull away from his hand, saying, "Because people are cruel and terrible in ways I want nothing to do with ever again. I, I need to go before I change my mind."

He lets his hand drop to his side, nodding. I turn and walk away before I can say anything else. Nims walks close beside me, bumping me as we walk. Resting my hand on her head I say to her, "I should have said no." She growls at me and I chuckle, "Ok, maybe I needed to say yes, but that doesn't make it less scary."

She bumps my leg with her shoulder as we arrive at the vampire bar. I don't really need to come here, but I enjoy it and I keep thinking that eventually I will meet some vampires. Well, more than just Bob, who tells me to stay away from the shifters and that vampires don't date shifters. And now I wonder why he said those things to me. As we enter, I notice Ailsa is over in the corner talking to some vampires. That's unusual.

It's not my business, so I shrug it off. Bob is sitting at the far end of the bar so I sit at the end closer to the door, Nims at my feet. The bartender brings me a rum and pineapple juice, my favorite drink. I have it every time I come here and since I don't actually drink anywhere else; I savor this one drink. The first sip is glorious, but I set the glass down faster when I hear Nims growl low and deep. Bob is seating himself on the next barstool over from me, saying, "Hi there Livi, how has your shopping trip been tonight?"

Moving my glass a little farther away from him, I say, "It was good. I wanted to be alone tonight, Bob. That's why I sat over here."

Something flashes across his face so quickly that I'm not sure what it is till he says, "You do? You smell like wolf. Is it just that you're a dirty wolf lover and don't want to hang around your own kind? Vampires not good enough for you?"

He gets louder as he talks, till he is practically shouting by the time he is asking if vampires are not good enough for me. Nims is growling and then another vampire is there behind Bob, snatching him up off the bar stool and walking him to the door. Bob protests the entire way, yelling that I'm a wolf lover and much worse. I barely even know him. Why would he care who I smell like? He is thrown out the door and the man doing the throwing tells him, "That was it, Bob. You can't come back in until you get Roman's permission. He said not to even ask for the next year. Maybe you should find a different region to haunt for a few hundred years."

He closes the door that had been standing open when I arrived and walks toward me. Ailsa appears on the other side of Nims. She startles me. Keeping my reaction contained, I say, "Hello Ailsa, fancy seeing you again tonight."

She snorts, "Indeed. As if you didn't notice me when you walked in the door. I've been talking with Roman over ther—," she glares at the man that just appeared at her side. "Olivia, this is Roman. Roman is the... head vampire for this area. Region, for this region. I have been discussing the man that has been following you with him."

Frowning, I say, "Why? I told you it's nothing. Probably there isn't really anyone following me."

Ailsa rolls her eyes, saying, "I remember very well what you said. But you are wrong. Someone is following you and they mean you harm. I want you safe and these guys are going to ensure you remain so, because you are important to me and my fellow witches."

Roman says, "You are a vampire in our region. It is our job to ensure that no harm comes to you and that no one reveals our presence while hunting you. The humans are particularly sensitive about us as it is. We don't need to start a war."

"What do you mean, start a war? That could happen? Just because they found out about us?"

Roman nods, telling me, "Yes, and that is why we take any threat seriously. In your case, there is the threat of exposure, but also the threat of pissing off all the witches."

Ailsa grins at him, saying, "You keep talking so sweet to me, and I'm going to think you've taken a liking to me, Roman."

Roman rolls his eyes, saying, "Not on my dumbest day would I think it would be a good idea for me to pursue you. I'd end up a frog and then the region would go to shit. Hard no from me. You're cute, but I don't fancy being a frog."

Ailsa's grin is impossibly wide and her eyes are twinkling as she says, "Oh no, there is no way I could fit your bulk into a frog. You would definitely have to be a boar. I'm told they are really quite smart, and very similar to humans."

Roman's eyes are mere slits as he says, "Thank you, no. I prefer my current form. Olivia, I am assigning Duncan," he gestures to the man standing next to me, "to stay with you. He is one of my Enforcers and very good at what he does."

"What exactly do you mean, stay with me?"

Ailsa chuckles as Roman says, "I mean, he will go where you go. He will stay where you stay. Until we have eliminated this threat. Ailsa, is she slow?"

Glaring at him, I say, "No! I am not slow! But I was hoping you meant something different. I don't want some man," looking over at Duncan I tell him, "apologies, I'm sure you are lovely to be around. I don't want to have some strange man following me around. What if the dogs don't like him? Nims is only one of my dogs. There are fifteen more at home, all in various stages of having been rescued. They might bite him. And, I am going out on my first date in over a decade, tomorrow night. A second guy tagging along is not especially good for a date last I checked."

Ailsa's eyes widen and she says, "He finally asked you?"

"You knew he was going to? Yes, he did." I look back at Roman, "I am certain I will be safe with him. What if I compromise a little? If I agree to have Duncan with me any other time I go out into the world, let him walk me home today and call before I go out again, that would allow you to still have your enforcer and me to have my privacy."

Roman shakes his head, saying, "I don't know. Who is this guy you are planning to go out with, anyway?"

"Blair, from the shop down the street."

Roman nods, "Ok. He is proficient. Very well. As long as you promise to only leave in the company of one of them. Ailsa, you ensure Blair is made aware of the situation?"

She nods, and I am mortified. I haven't even had the chance to embarrass myself during our date. It's going to happen before I can fuck anything up. Super. "I would rather be the one to tell him. Duncan here can wait outside while I let Blair know, in case maybe he wants to cancel."

Roman nods, "Very well."

Seven

Olivia

I can't believe he still wants to take me out tomorrow. Even walked with me to make sure I got to Duncan with no issue. What is this world I am living in? People just don't go out of their way for others like this, even when it benefits them slightly. They could have simply killed me and been done with the problem that is being caused by my presence. Or told me to leave. The latter is a lot more appealing to me, but the first option was my death.

I've been watching Duncan surreptitiously as we walk. He is tall, pale, and reddish. His hair is a chestnut color, and there are some red highlights in different lights. His eyes are the color of dark honey. He looks more solid than extra muscled. He is attractive over all, physically. Not a word from him since he threw Bob out of the bar, so for all I know, he isn't smart enough to carry a conversation. Or maybe he thinks I am annoying, and he is just pissed that he has to walk me home.

Latching on to that idea, I say, "You know, you could just go back. I'll swear you walked me all the way home. I am really sorry they made you do this."

He glances at me, a twist in his full lips. As he continues scanning the area we are walking through, he says, "I don't mind walking you home. I mind you suggesting I skip out on my duty. And I think we are about to have company. There are two men following behind us. Keep walking." Nims growls low, and Duncan says, "And two more to your right. I would bet that another two will come at us from the next side road. How are you at fighting?"

"Better than I was, but not six men by myself good."

He says, "Fair enough, most people aren't without a lot of practice. What is the silver thing they are carrying? Every one of them has a silver handle strapped to them. Are they carrying knives?"

Wincing, I say, "No. Those are exactly the people I thought I left behind. Those are crosses. They think I am a demon and they are going to kill me by stabbing me with one of those silver crosses. Probably going to kill you, too."

We are steps away from the place where another road connects to this one. Duncan tells me, "Stay loose, be ready. The other four are closing in."

Whispering, I tell Nims, "I love you Nims. We'll get through this one too." She bumps my thigh with her head and I reach down like I am going to give her a scratch. Instead, I unhook her harness and let it drop to the ground.

They won't use something I put on her to hold her while they hurt her.

I hear someone shout now and all hell breaks loose. A man grabs me from behind and screams in fear as he flies over my head. I see three of the men fighting with Duncan and I turn to my Nims. She is holding two of them off, growling and snapping at them. They are trying to circle around behind her, but she isn't having it. I step up next to her and the men smile. The one on the left says, "Hey, pretty lady, why don't you call off your dog and we'll all go talk. It'll be fun. I promise."

I cringe at his words, "Have you no shame? That was so cheesy the seventies called to ask if you'd like to read lines for a special movie."

The man that spoke is mad now and rushes at me. As soon as the hand with that awful, sharpened silver cross is in reach, I grab it and snatch him toward the ground. The cross clatters noisily as he hits the ground. Kicking his ribs, the sound of them cracking is music to my ears. He howls with pain and I kick him in the head. I know we don't want any company of the human sort right now. Nims is growling and the other man is shouting his head off. She has him by the arm and is slinging him around.

Picking up the cross the other man dropped, I hold the sharp end and wait for her to swing him towards me. As soon as he gets within reach, I give his brain pan a little tap with the handle. The tap sounds louder than I think it should have, and he drops like a sack of potatoes. Nims spits his arm out like it tasted bad and we turn in time to see Duncan throw the last man he was fighting against a wall. The sound is disturbing, a sort of wet crunch, and he leaves a dark stain as he slides to the ground.

Duncan turns to us, asking, "Are you both all right?" We nod and he pulls out his phone as he says, "I need to call some people to clean this up. Get over here into the shadows near the wall, so you are less visible. They aren't looking for me." Nims and I do as he said, while he taps the screen of his phone a couple times and puts it to his ear. I can't hear exactly what he is saying. He is working to muffle his voice. He knows how sensitive vampire ears are. I can only guess that he spent some time figuring out how to avoid being heard when he wants to have a private conversation.

It makes no sense for him to keep this conversation private when I know very well it is mostly about me and the attack. His call ends and he glares at his phone for a moment before putting it back in his pocket. He looks at me and says, "Come on, let's go." As we walk toward my home, he says, "I've been ordered to stay with you."

"What? No! You can't! I didn't agree to this!"

He holds up a hand, saying, "I know. I was there for the agreement. But that was before you — we, were attacked on the way to your house by a group of men. If it helps you to be more comfortable with it, I'm not happy about it either."

"No! It doesn't help at all. Great. Just fucking great. What if the other dogs don't like you? If you hit my dogs, I'm hitting you. I don't care if they bite you. You aren't supposed to be coming to stay at my house. You know what? I won't have it. That's it. You just can't."

He sighs and says, "I am staying at your house or I am

taking you to mine. I will not defy my principal just so you can be more comfortable."

"I don't give a fuck about your principal, and you can tell him I said that. You are not staying at my house and I sure as fuck am not going to yours. That's final. I don't care what you tell them, but I am sticking to the original agreement."

He makes a strangled sort of growling sound and says, "You are entirely too important to the community for us to allow you to remain unprotected while you are under threat."

My heart freezes in my chest. Oh no. I can't be important to these people. No. Oh no, no, no. How did this happen? I kept my distance, dammit. I can't have these people caring about me; considering me important to the community. Fucking hell. Turning, I start walking toward the house. Nims is at my side and he is there on the other side before I get two steps away. I know he is waiting for more of an argument. I have nothing after that bomb he dropped on me.

Duncan

I won. Holy shit. She just let it go and started walking home. Is this a trick? Why did she look like I killed her mom when I told her she was important to the community? It doesn't matter; she is going along with it now and that is what I needed her to do. Nims is looking at me as we walk. There is something strange about that dog. Not that it is strange that she stayed with Olivia to fight. No, that was the most normal thing about the dog.

She looks like she is listening all the time. I know she is judging me. That is written all over her face in the way her jowls tighten and her eyes narrow. The way she fought alongside Olivia, it just isn't natural for a dog. She also didn't lose control the way a dog usually would while trying to protect their person.

It doesn't seem possible that she trained the dog to fight with her. She already admitted to not being great at it. Something about that dog... Her house is dark, but I can smell that she has several dogs in there. Dogs whose nails I can hear clicking across floors as they wake up and realize that she is home. Olivia stops, looking back at me as she is half thru the door, saying, "You are invited in Duncan."

Does she really not know that we don't need an invitation to come in a home? What does she know about being a vampire if she thinks we need to be invited into a place? Who taught her that? I need to find out who her maker is. Does she have a family? And if she doesn't, who is responsible for that? Turning a new vampire loose on the world with no training is a crime.

The dogs are all sitting in the entry, waiting for her to greet them. While she greets each of the fifteen dogs individually, they all watch me. I have the distinct feeling that they would not hesitate to bite the hell out of me if I were to distress her in any way. I ask her, "Have you not had luck in adopting them out lately?"

She pauses in her greetings to say, "I never have a problem finding them a suitable home when they are ready.

The reason is that currently there are a great many more dogs in need. They stay here until they can trust people again. For some," she gestures toward a dog on the far left, "it takes years. And others," she gestures toward a dog to the right of the first, "will probably never again trust humans. When I found that one, she was mostly starved and had been viciously beaten. It looked like another dog had chewed her. If I hadn't had Nims with me that day, she would have run away from me. As it was, I sent Nims to over to convince her to give me a chance. I don't know how she does it. She always manages to convince them and they come along with us, even if they can't look directly at me for the first few months they are here. So she will likely spend the rest of her life with us. Others, like this little guy in front of me, he will meet his first person soon. I have a waiting list of people that want one of my dogs. They can only get on my list by word of mouth. Someone has to recommend them. Even after they are recommended, I watch them for a time. If they make it through that, then they get put on the list. They don't get to choose the dog. The dog chooses them."

"How long have you been rescuing dogs?"

She sighs, saying, "About five years. That was when I got into a financial situation that allowed me to do this." She stands after greeting the last dog and says, "Come. I'll give you a tour and then I need to work."

As I follow, I ask her, "What do you do for work?"

She raises a brow and leads me further into the house as she says, "I write horror novels where the men always die. Here is the living room, we don't use it much but you are welcome to. Across the hall is my office. I ask that you stay out of there. Unless you have come in to speak to me, but try to avoid that or I am putting you in a book and murdering you in the most gruesome manner I can think of."

Her tour is interesting. The house is decorated in darker tones. Lots of dark wood and dark furniture. The house is older while the furniture is newer. There are things on the wall, but no pictures of people. No family, no friends. She does have pictures of her and Nims. The is one in the hall near the kitchen that is haunting. It looks like they were camping and she took a selfie of the two of them. It's her eyes though, it looks like she was hanging on by a thread and Nims looks like she knew it. She is just behind Olivia with her head resting on her shoulder. Her eyes are dark and her face grim. Her stance looks tight, like she is on guard, though the head resting on Olivia's shoulder would suggest ease and comfort. I ask her, "Hey, when was this picture taken?" Happily, I stopped myself from asking why they look so broken in it.

She walks back across the kitchen and looks at the picture. A sad smile crosses her lips and she says, "That was about ten years ago." She turns away and starts back across the kitchen, all the dogs trailing her, "Come on, I'll show you where I keep the stores. In case you are hungry."

With one last look at the picture that will probably haunt me, I turn and follow her. I see the last of the dogs following her down the stairs into the basement. Whoa. She has a lot of synthetic blood stored here. Turning a slow circle, I ask her, "Why is there so much?"

She shrugs, and says, "I just want to make sure I don't run out. Plus, the witches think I don't eat enough. They usually slip in an extra bag or two. Let's head upstairs so you can pick your room."

Looking around as I follow her, I have so many questions. Why does she have so much blood stockpiled? What happened to them before she took that picture? How did she get to this point without a family? What the fuck is up with her dog staring me down when I lag because I am looking at her house or walking slowly?

She shows me three bedrooms. I choose the one decorated in shades of brown. It feels more inviting to me than the green or the blue. She points to the door at the end of the hall, "That is my room. Please do not go in there unless I invite you."

"Yes, I imagine I wouldn't get far anyway with all your guardians underfoot." She laughs, and the sound is music to my ears. Her smile lights up her face for the short time it is there. I want to see her smile again, that smile. It is magnetic. It draws me in and I just want to keep her close and make her smile all the time. Whoa, that's not a train of thought I need to follow.

She is already turning to leave; the smile gone like it never was and the room seems a little darker without it.

Olivia

As I walk away from the room he has chosen, I remember that tonight is hunting night. Stopping, I turn and call out to him, "I just remembered I have to take the dogs out. Tonight is hunting night. I'll be back soon."

He is in the hall before I finish my sentence, and he is

shirtless. Wow! That is a lot of chiseled for one chest and certainly more than I have ever seen. Oh my. Is it hot in here? I think it's hot in here. Focus Olivia, focus.

He is frowning over all those abs as he says, "You can't go out by yourself. I don't know that it is a really great idea for you to go out at all tonight as the people after you have already attacked us once. What if they bring reinforcements?"

Shrugging, I tell him, "I won't be alone. I'll have sixteen dogs with me that are there specifically to hunt something. They aren't real particular. It's me that says they can only hunt deer."

He pinches the bridge of his nose, eyes closed and sighs. I'd probably be more annoyed if he didn't have all that chest and those abs out distracting me. He says, "The dogs don't count as you not being alone. At the very least, I need to come with you."

Great, that's just what I need. Abs here wandering about while I try to hunt. "Are you quite sure? I mean, I am taking fifteen dogs. I feel like that equals at least one annoying vampire."

He chuckles, "Annoying, eh? The dogs would no doubt do really well. But they don't have the healing capacity that vampires have. If I get stabbed by one of those weird crosses, I'm just going to be mad. Your dogs will be injured badly. I know you would not want that."

Well, that's hitting below the belt. Resigned, I tell him, "Fine, you can tag along. But don't get in the way of our hunt. And go put a shirt on for fuck's sake." His low chuckle does spicy things to me as I walk away from him to get the dogs ready to go. I don't need this.

Eight

Duncan

I can feel their disapproving stares boring into the back of my head. I don't know what dog was supposed to sit in the front seat tonight, but they are all unhappy that I usurped their coveted seat. Luckily, the drive is short. As soon as Olivia puts the vehicle in park, I get out and open the back door to let the dogs out. My hopes for the dogs forgiving me were quickly dashed as they all ignored me while exiting the vehicle in the most orderly manner I have ever seen for this number of dogs. Especially considering how excited they must be on hunting night. These have got to be the weirdest strays I have ever seen in my life. Looking over at Olivia, I can see her pride in the dogs' behavior.

She really is fascinating. How has she managed all this time? She is so strong, to be living away from her vampire family. I need to ask her about that. Maybe while we follow the dogs?

They start for the woods and I realize I am holding the door open for no one. With a shove, I close the door and run over to catch up. As I slow next to her, I step on a stick that breaks with the loudest sound I have ever heard a stick make, and everyone turns their head to look at me. I didn't know dogs' faces could be so disapproving. Olivia whisper yells at me, "This is a hunt. If you cannot be quiet like everyone else, you can wait at the vehicle. The dogs wait for this hunt all week, and even the puppies are quieter than you."

Adding insult to my injury, Nims snorts at me and leads the other dogs further into the woods. Watching Nims disappear into the woods, I tell Olivia, "I am not waiting at the car. That's out of the question." Following her carefully, I ask, "What's up with your dog, anyway?"

Her glare as she turns to look at me in the darkness is furious, "There is nothing up with my Nims. She just thinks you are dumb. Can you not tell that from her facial expression? In case you can't tell from mine, I think you are dumb too. As well as entirely to impressed with yourself. Now zip it so my puppies can enjoy their hunt."

She brushes past me, her anger palpable as she picks her way through the forest. How is she stomping through and still so silent? The hunt commences and I can't help but to be awed as they choose their mark and bring down the deer. Once they have downed it, Olivia kisses its forehead and then quickly breaks its neck, ending the creature's suffering. She pulls out a bag and rope from her pockets. I can only guess that the witches provided these things as they grow once freed from her pockets.

With practiced moves, she gets the deer hung from the branch and the bag attached to the deer. She pulls a knife from an inside pocket of her jacket and reaches into the bag, cutting the deer's throat. "Why are you doing that? Can you not drink directly from the deer?"

She and Nims turn their heads to look at me like I am the dumbest creature to walk the planet. Olivia says, "Did you never think about how the witches create all the synthetic blood we drink? They still need actual blood to create it. We have a deal now. I provide them with fresh blood and they pay me. It's been very lucrative, and I think they may have cornered the market for our area because of it."

"How did you come up with that? I've been here for a few hundred years and I never realized they needed some fresh to start with. I am impressed."

She shrugs, "I don't know. Maybe I am just nosy. Maybe I thought about it because I haven't been around for a few hundred years and I still wonder about things."

I grab my chest like she shot me, "Oh, ouch! Shots fired, I'm hit. Ok. So you get curious. Did you just wander into the witch's shop and ask them? Say, how do you make the synthetic stuff?"

She shrugs while sealing the bag. As she eases the carcass to the ground, she says, "I did, actually. They have always been really nice to me." Turning toward me, she says, "Can you wait just here with the dogs? I need to leave this carcass over by the cat's den but, if they smell you, they won't come near it. It took six months of leaving the carcass closer and closer before they would look at something I offered them."

I don't like it. She is probably safe enough out here, though. "Sure, yes, go ahead. Just don't be long or me and the dogs are coming over there."

She chuckles, a low throaty sound that sends a shot of

lust directly to my dick. I do not need this right now. Especially not while that ass is walking off through the woods with a deer carcass over her shoulder and Nims at her side. I want to peel that clothing off her and see what other sexy little sounds she makes. No! No. I do not want that. I want to do my job and keep the secret of vampires and other creatures safe from the humans. That's it. Olivia is a complication I do not need in my life. Period.

She and Nims come walking back, silent as mice. She lifts the bag of blood and snaps her fingers. All the dogs head back for the vehicle. She taps a spot on the bag and it shrinks down to barely fill her hand. I ask her, "Can you put it in your pocket like that?"

She starts toward the vehicle, saying, "No. When it is full and shrunken, it cannot be squished or the blood inside will start coming out and rapidly returning to its full volume. Happily, they made sure I knew about that before I found out the hard way."

"That could have been a rather colossal mess. Do you hang on to that until the next time you go to the market? Pop it into your basement storage?"

She closes the door to the vehicle after Nims steps in and opens hers while saying, "No. The blood needs to be fresh. The only way it stays as fresh as they want it is if it continues circulating. A temporary ride in the bag is no problem. But a week? That would be. They have a spot behind the market that I take it to and empty the bag. I don't know where it goes after that but, it isn't my business and I don't worry about it."

She's started the vehicle and got us heading for the market, even as she explains this to me. I think she would have left me in the woods had I not got in when she did, so I could hear the rest of her story. "How, um, how did you become a vampire?"

She frowns, "I was nearly dead, and a vampire gave me his blood."

Gave? "Wait, he didn't bite you?"

"No, I was pretty well dying when he found me."

"Okay, well, then what? Did he bring you home to meet the family?"

"Ha, that's a thing?"

"Yes, that's a thing. Did he not do that?"

She shrugs, a casual lift and drop of one shoulder, "No. There were... some complications and I couldn't leave right then. He said he would find me the next evening, but he never did. Might have made things easier if he had."

"It certainly would have. Newly turned are supposed to stay in the charge of their maker for the first five years. That's why we have such stringent laws about making sure the one being turned fully understands what will happen to them and what will be required of them, all the commitments they are signing up for in becoming a vampire."

Her frown grows deeper as she puts the vehicle in park, "We're supposed to consent to this? I didn't even know exactly what was happening to me for the first few weeks. It, it was a frightening time. Sit here. I won't be long and I don't think I need to worry about the humans coming after me here."

I nod, speechless. She figured this out by herself? I mean, not everything because there are some definite gaps in her vampire laws knowledge, along with any knowledge of the agreement that must be made before one is turned.

How was she nearly dead? I completely understand why the vampire would want to save her but, is it worth his life and his family's reputation? What was he thinking? I watch as she gets back in the vehicle. Waiting until she is driving us back to her house to ask one more burning question, "Do you know who it was that turned you?"

She shrugs again, "No, he didn't give me a name that I remember. But I was still more than a little wooden headed from the near death experience."

We sit in silence for the rest of the drive. Once we all get inside, she takes the dogs into the office with her. Standing there with the doorknob in her hand, she tells me, "You have the run of the house. Just stay out of my room, that's creepy. And please do not interrupt me while I am working, thanks."

She shuts the door before I can respond. Oh well. Guess I with check the rest of the house, make sure things are locked. Wandering through the house, I can't help but notice how the decor gives a window into her life. It's all greens and darker earth tones down here. She has a picture feature wall in each room filled with old pictures of families.

Every room has seating for multiple people that look as though they have been used very little and only by her. Even the table in the kitchen has five chairs. So far I found two windows unlocked and fixed that. Opening the kitchen door that leads to the backyard, I smell something. Closing the door behind me, I step out into the darkness beyond the glow of the porch light. My eyes adjust fast, allowing me to walk the perimeter of the fenced area. There isn't anyone here, that much I can smell. But it smells like meat? She doesn't feed the dogs raw meat... I see the meat now.

Chunks, like what would be put into a stew tossed over the fence. Fucking hell.

What kind of bastards try to kill dogs? Crossing the yard, I fetch a bowl and some napkins from inside. Bringing them back out, I begin the process of picking up all the little pieces of tainted meat, making sure I get every single piece. Nobody needs a woman that loves dogs as much as she does crazy with grief and looking for revenge. Who knows what the fuck she would do? All the meat picked up, I head back inside.

Tossing the napkins into the garbage as I pass through the kitchen, it doesn't take long for me to pick them up after they do not make it in the can. Pushing the lid and making sure they go in, I continue on toward her office with the bowl of tainted meat in tow.

Olivia

The killer has to murder this guy, but where is he going to catch—my train of thought is completely derailed when he knocks on the door. Every dog in the room lifts their head and stares at the door. I raise my voice to be heard through the door, "Go away. I am working."

He knocks again. This time saying, "I think you need to see this."

With a groan, I tell him, "Fine. Come in. But watch where you step!" When he opens the door, he stops mid-step and just looks around my office. A sudden case of nerves has me taking a closer look at it. Dog beds everywhere. My big desk is in the middle of the room, all dark wood and bulk. The many balls of fur everywhere because I haven't vacuumed today, and it is always blowout season for the dogs, it seems. The couple sets of shelves crammed with books. And not much else. I have barely done anything in this room but write. I didn't even paint the walls, they are still the boring eggshell they were when I moved in. Shame for the way my office looks burns through me and I snap at him, "Did you only want to stare at my office? I assure you, I didn't need to see that."

He frowns at me and I notice he has a bowl in his hand. He picks his way through the dogs and sets the bowl on my desk, saying, "I was just a little surprised at the room, that's all. This," he points at the bowl, "is what you needed to see. I found it outside."

Frowning, I look at the bowl. Chunks of meat? He found meat outside? A dark suspicion crawls up my spine and stabs my heart with fear. Looking up at him, his face confirms the fear spiking through me. As I stand I say, "How fucking dare they! Who would do something so horrible? Why would anyone try to hurt my dogs? They've done nothing to anyone!"

He nods, asking, "Do you know of anyone that might still hold a grudge? Maybe someone from your past?"

I start to shake my head when I remember the white spots on their collars. Could he still be chasing me? "I need some tea. I'll tell you while the kettle heats." Dashing out of the room, I leave him to follow or not. I just feel like I don't have any air and I need tea. I need the ritual of tea. Grabbing the kettle, I fill it and set it on the stove. Nims made it into the kitchen while I was filling the kettle. I hear him pull out a chair to sit and spin to face him, "Do you want some?"

He swallows and carefully says, "I'm sorry. I don't think I have the full picture?"

"Tea? Do you want some damn tea? What the fuck else would I — oh for fucks sake. I'm not asking if you want that. Would you like some tea?"

The smirk on his face makes me want to slap him and crawl into his lap. I don't like it. He says, "Yes, I would like some tea, thank you. Whatever you are having will be fine."

Rolling my eyes at him, I turn back to the cabinets. Pulling out two cups and setting them next to the stove. Then I move to my little happy set of drawers. It looks like a small section of a really old card catalog from a library. Nine drawers, all square and the perfect size for my tea bags. Opening them one by one and smelling the fragrance released is soothing. It gives my brain the space to remember the way the preacher hunted me. The look in his eyes the few times he nearly caught me. That black suit he always wore with the small square of white showing at the throat. The cross that was always strapped to his side, shiny and silver.

The kettle whistles, bringing me back to now. Grabbing two tea bags, I close the drawer and cross to the stove, to press the button that releases the cap on the spout that makes the noise. In the silence that follows, I lean on the ritual of placing the bags in the cups, filling them with the hot water, and inhaling the scent that wafts up.

I have nothing left with which to put this off, so I pick up the cups and walk over to the table. Setting them down, I pull out a chair and seat myself as I push a cup toward him.

I put my hands around the cup, soaking up the warmth as I say, "When I was first turned, I didn't know what the hell was happening to me. I didn't have anyone to answer questions or help me. So I called my best friends over. It… It went poorly. They ran out and left me to close a door that the sun was beaming through. Apparently, they went directly to my parents. My parents brought the pastor over with them. They wanted me to allow him to perform an exorcism—"

"A what?" He holds up a hand, "Are you telling me you were in distress and the first thing your parents did was try to subject you to an exorcism?"

Nodding, I tell him, "Yes. That's exactly what they did."

He shakes his head, "I mean this with all disrespect to their names, fuck them. I apologize if you are somehow still on speaking terms with them and my sentiment offends you."

"While I appreciate the apology, it is unnecessary. When I refused the exorcism, they disowned me." His face is a little scary looking right now, but if I stop, I won't be able to tell him. Sighing, I say, "When I left the area not long after that, the preacher tracked me down and tried to force me to submit to an exorcism. Over and over again. He was the reason I left the US and still he hunted me through quite a few European countries. I finally lost him when I went off grid for a while, just walked into the woods one day and stayed wandering in the woods for a while. When I came out, I was in a different country than when I had gone in. But he wasn't there. That was around eight years ago. I haven't seen him, or anyone like him, since. Until tonight."

His voice is gruff as he asks, "How long did you say it

was since you were turned?"

With a shrug, I say, "Ten years, give or take a few months." My tea cup is super interesting to look at while he does that math. He growls and I look up, "I didn't know vampires growl. Is that a male vampire thing?"

He shakes his head no and gingerly lifts his cup to take a sip. His hands are shaking a little, but he doesn't spill anything. "Are you all right?"

Setting his cup down ever so carefully, he says, "Yes, I am all right. I am angry on your behalf, but all right. Vampires do not necessarily growl, but I do when I am angry. Let me see if I am reading into your story correctly, if you don't mind?" I shake my head no and he continues, "You grew up in a religious home. As a young adult, you were living on your own when you were turned under odd circumstances. Your parents brought a priest over when you were reported to have behaved oddly, and they wanted you to give permission for an exorcism. When you said no, they disowned you and the preacher spent around two years hunting you until you disappeared into the woods. Do I have the general idea?"

"Yes, that fairly sums it up. They thought I had a demon in me."

He nods and asks, "What is the name of your parents' church? And that preacher. What is his name?"

"The church is the Southich Baptist. The preacher's name is Malleus Kramer."

His face suddenly changes, and he shouts as he runs over and grabs me. He shoves me behind him and says, "Who the fuck are you?"

"We live here. Who are you?"

Nine

Olivia

He just had to involve the dogs. As soon as they heard him shout, the rest of the dogs came charging at full volume into the kitchen. The noise was deafening until I shouted, "Silence!" All the dogs went quiet, even Nims. She had a low growl going from where she had wedged herself between Duncan and I. He is still holding onto my arm, "Let go of me. I can't very well tell you if they are someone that should be here if all I can see is your back!" His hand releases its grip on my arm and I straighten. Nims crowds into me, pressing me a little further back from him, so I put a hand on her head to comfort her while I lean out to look around Duncan and see the ghosts. Oh super. "Duncan, you have just protected me from the ghosts that were here long before I bought this place. They can be annoying and pompous, but are not, in fact, harmful." Stepping out from behind him, I ask them, "What are you doing? I've told you not to scare people. Do you need something?"

Ralph, the super pompous asshole that apparently was

murdered by his dear wife Sara for things she won't speak of, twists his lips up and snidely says, "The holy men are finally coming to get you, we have no reason to concern ourselves with your proprieties any longer. We'll be running this house once again and everything will be as it should be."

"What did you say?"

He sneers at me, "You heard me! This will be a good, God-fearing home once again! All your evil will be gone after the holy men take you away and cleanse this place of your taint."

I can feel a rage rising in me as dots start connecting. In case I am wrong, I ask, "You saw them? Were they the ones that threw the poisoned meat over the fence?"

Sara nods, saying, "Oh yes, that really was ill-done of them. They said something about you having too many dogs and they needed to thin the herd."

The bubble of rage explodes and I shout at them, "Are you fucking kidding me? Why wouldn't you tell me? If not about them being holy men, at the very least to save the lives of the dogs! You should have told me about the poisoned meat! All of you get to the damned attic or I swear to fuck I am burning juniper every damn day! Better yet, I'll get the witches in here and they can shove you in a jar. You can do their bidding and stop bothering me!" The ghosts are gone before I finish, but I know they heard me anyway. Looking over at Duncan, I say, "Fine. I obviously have some idiots after me of the holier-than-thou variety. What do I do? Would moving again do the trick? Because I am definitely going to outlive them, right?"

He runs a hand down his face, "Yes, that is technically an option. But it would cause problems for everyone."

My brows drop and I ask, "What do you mean? How would that cause problems for anyone but me?"

He sits heavily, "If you move, it will seriously piss off the witches. They do business with you, yes, and they would not want to lose that. More importantly, they like you. They want you around, which is why they came and told us to take care of your issues. They did this, not because they didn't feel like they could handle the issue, but because we would lose face if they did it. It is only courtesy that prompted them to let us handle it. If you were to complain about your ghosts to them, you would find that suddenly they were gone. And you would never be bothered by them again. They care about you and would be sad to lose you."

All the air is gone from the room suddenly. My knees give out, leaving me sitting on the floor, Nims pressing against me.

* * *

Duncan

She looks so broken at the idea of people caring for her. I want to comfort her but the instant I move Nims is staring daggers at me. There is something really strange about that dog. Something tickling the back of my mind... vampire dogs. She doesn't seem like the ones we had to put down. She is very in control, nowhere near rabid. I haven't seen her go on any killing sprees. And I know she has wanted to kill me a few times. She and Olivia have a deep love for each other. That dog would definitely die for her. If she is a vampire dog, we have a problem. The law says we must put vampire dogs to death. If we put that dog to death, either we are going to have to put Olivia to death with her or she will die trying to stop it.

If either of them dies, the witches are going to start a war. They would burn it all to the ground and kill every single vampire in the region if Olivia dies. I have got to call Roman. Nims gives her a little nudge with her nose and she presses her face into the dog's fur. Shortly after, she stands and faces me, saying, "I think perhaps you are mistaken. They would just miss the ready availability of the blood, that's all." I cannot believe her. How is it possible she thinks this? I look at Nims and I would swear she shrugged at me. But, that isn't possible, right? Olivia clears her throat and says, "Moving away doesn't seem to be the preferred option, so what do you suggest?"

Deciding to leave that mess alone, I go with the current plan. Taking a breath, I say, "For now, I stay here with you because neither of us really has a choice in that. If I leave and you are kidnapped or killed, it won't go well for me. I was ordered to stay with you. I will talk to Roman later and see if anything is going to change. What about your family? Do they know you are here?"

Her brows drop and her mouth purses a little, "Wha— what do you mean, my family? We talked about them. I have nothing to do with my parents."

"No, your vampire — that's right, you don't have a vampire family."

She shrugs, "No. I don't even know the name of the one that turned me. It was... a chaotic night. Like I told you, he didn't stick around."

"I can't imagine why anyone would flout the law like that. It's nearly morning. Why don't you get some rest and

I'll work on some things while I keep an eye out for the guys trying to kill you."

She narrows her eyes at me, "Don't you need to rest too?"

"No. The older you get, the less sleep you need. I can stay awake for a week or so before I start to yawn."

"Super. I am going to bed. Puppies, come." I watch as the dogs file out behind her and Nims.

Ten

Duncan

I wait for the sounds from upstairs to fade away. It doesn't take long. She was probably a lot more tired than she let on. Standing, I wander toward the front of the house and close myself into what would have been a drawing room in years past. Pulling my phone out, I tap the screen and call Roman. It rings once and he answers.

"What have you learned?"

Pacing the floor, I start with her family, saying, "I learned she doesn't know who her family is. Whoever it was that turned her, they didn't stick around. She says that the guy said he would find her the next day, but she's never seen him again." I go on to tell him about her parent's church and how we are pretty certain that they are who is after her. "But none of that even comes close to this last part."

Roman groans, "What do you mean none of this comes close? She has a damned church after her!"

"I think the dog is a vampire, too."

"You're shitting me. No way has that dog been all over

town all this time and a fucking vampire. You know they go rabid over it."

Shoving a hand through my hair to get it out of my face, I say, "I know! But this dog isn't normal. If my calculations are right, that dog is over ten years old. You know we rarely have dogs, especially the large breeds. Their life spans are so short... This dog doesn't act like she has aged. She fought side by side with Olivia when we were attacked on the way home and walked away uninjured."

The phone clatters. I'm pretty certain Roman dropped it. Sure of it when I hear his hand scrabbling to pick it up, "Has she attacked anyone? Does she seem feral at all?"

"No, and no. She seems incredibly intelligent and empathetic. Very protective of Olivia. She loves her more than anything. She helps her with the other dogs. What if, what if it's the bond between them that keeps her from going feral? What if that was what that fool that was killed by his hunting dogs was missing?"

Roman swears viciously, then says, "I don't fucking care how that idiot died. I sincerely hope you are wrong. Because you know who else the witches really fucking like? The damned dog! Fucking Ailsa, the head fucking witch of the entire country, told me herself that both of them better be well protected. She also said that if it looked like we couldn't do it, they would take her in and claim her as one of their family. We cannot let that happen. The loss of prestige is something our region can ill afford with how strangely the council has been acting. You make sure her and that damn dog stay safe. I don't care what you have to do. Keep them safe. And talk to her about the damn dog, find out how the fuck that shit happened. Did she turn the dog? She doesn't have any family. Does she know how dangerous it is for anyone to find out about the dog? I want to know immediately after you get confirmation. I need to know how hot the damn water is before anything else happens."

I agree, and Roman ends the call as he says he needs a drink. Taking a breath, I collect my thoughts and roll my shoulders. We'll get through this. Our family is strong, and we have weathered worse. The vampire world isn't exactly known for its lack of intrigue. Opening the door and stepping into the hall, I stop as I hear a sound from the kitchen. It isn't loud, but there should be no sounds from there. Stuffing my phone in my pocket, I step softly toward the kitchen. As I draw near the doorway, I lean toward the middle of the hallway so that I can see into the kitchen. Two men in the same garb as the ones from earlier. They look like preachers with strange holsters for large, silver crosses.

Gathering myself, I race into the kitchen, punching one in the side of the head to take him out of the equation. Before the man hits the floor, I have the other one by the throat and, holding him close to me, I ask, "Who are you?" I feel the blade sink into my side. If I were mortal, that would be problematic. As a vampire, one stab wound will be gone quickly enough, so I smile at him. He looks terrified as I move him a little farther away from me. He pisses himself as I pull his knife out of my body and lick the blood off the blade. I ask him again, "Who are you?"

He sputters a bit before he finally says, "Nobody! Just a flunkie sent to retrieve a stupid girl! Please let me go! I swear, I swear I'll never come back."

He is crying and pleading. His piss smells foul. I need information, so I ask him, "Who sent you?"

He is crying as he says, "Southich Baptist Organization. They want the girl. That's all I know, I swear."

I smile down at him, "That's good enough." He closes his eyes in relief, as if he thinks I will release him because he's done well. My teeth sink into the soft skin of his neck and he stiffens briefly, like he would fight the inevitable. Once he is drained, I drop his body. Looking at the other one, I can see his chest rising and falling at a measured pace. Good. I'll tell the cleanup crew to drop him off with the witches. A gift of goodwill.

Eleven

Olivia

Opening my eyes, the first thing I see are the dogs all staring at me. Did I oversleep? My phone says no. Maybe they are just really ready to go outside. "Okay, okay. I'm up. Let me get dressed and we'll go outside. Don't forget the new rules. Nobody eats anything I didn't give them." A quick trip to my bathroom and then to the closet for fresh yoga pants and shirt has me opening the bedroom door to head downstairs. Halfway down the stairs, I smell the blood. Nims smells it too and picks up her pace to get into the kitchen. When I get in there, all the dogs are sitting at the door waiting, except Nims. She is sitting in the kitchen doorway looking at Duncan.

My kitchen looks as it should, so I ask him, "Why does the kitchen smell like someone bled here?"

He looks up from his cup and says, "Two men from the Southich Baptist Church stopped by today after you went to bed."

"Dammit. Do I need to worry about anything being in the yard?"

He shakes his head no, saying, "I've had it checked by the cleanup crew."

With a nod, I walk over and open the door for the dogs to go outside. I just leave it open so I can hear anything that happens out there. I work at making my evening coffee as my mind races. Why are they back? What the hell am I going to do? How do I get rid of them for good? I feel it when Nims comes back in. Her fur is speckled with morning mist and chilled from the air outside. The other dogs come parading in and I start the process of feeding everyone. Nims' dish gets some blood mixed in most days, but I don't feel comfortable doing that with him watching. After they are fed and returning outside to take care of other business, I sit at the table with my coffee. Duncan looks at me. I am ready to squirm under his gaze when he says, "Is Nims a vampire too?"

Nims stands next to me and I put an arm around her, saying, "She is. Why?"

He groans and asks, "Do you know anything about vampire laws? No, of course you don't. How would you? Dogs being turned is strictly forbidden."

I feel panic rising in my chest, "What happens to dogs that have been turned?"

He stares into his cup as he murmurs, "We kill them." Looking back up, he speaks fast, "The only vampire that ever turned dogs on purpose was immediately killed by those dogs. We have believed all this time that dogs immediately go feral when they are turned."

Hugging her closer, I tell him, "My Nims is not feral!

She is amazing. I don't know what I would do without her." Pressing my face against Nims face, I say, "I don't know if I could live in a world that didn't include her."

He nods, "I've seen that Nims is nothing like a feral animal. Anyone with eyes can see the love between the two of you. The bond. She seems nearly human. The problem is that if vampires notice how Nims behaves, or that she is over ten years old, they are going to realize that she isn't normal. If they notice the same behaviors that I noticed, her life will be in danger. Which puts you in danger."

"You're damn right it does, because no one is taking her from me."

He sighs, "I know. And Roman knows. We want to help you keep her alive. Nims, that means you have to act more like one of these dogs." He gestures around the room at the other dogs that have come back inside to sprawl across the floor. I look over at the door and see that one of the dogs has nudged it closed. He continues, "That means you need to bark sometimes, like one of them would." She barks right then, a deep, throaty bark that causes him to jump and glare at her. Her lips curve up into a doggy smile and I am left struggling to contain my laughter. Duncan changes the subject, telling me about the men that broke in last night.

He says that they are supposed to collect me and I tell him, "They probably still want to perform an exorcism on me." I have zero intentions of telling him or anyone else what I think the preacher might also want to do to me. That is something I hope to never give him the power over me to enact. Nims pokes me in the shoulder with her nose. I look at her, "What?" She tips her head briefly toward

Duncan and then stares me in the eyes. "He doesn't need to know about that. It isn't pertinent."

She lets out a little "Woof" at me, and Duncan chuckles. He says, "You may as well tell me, she has decided."

"Fine," I say before I tell him about the way the preacher always smelled like he was turned on, how his eyes were never where they should be, how the pitch of his voice spoke of his excitement over the idea of having me in his power. It leaves me feeling slimy just talking about it. Nims pokes me again and gives me that glare, so I continue on to tell him that he had been staring at me for much longer than that. "There was one other thing. We were there for one of the exorcisms. And that was horrible enough, but before he started, he looked at her and me standing with my parents on the other side of her. He said that it did not surprise him that the devil wanted one of the offerings. I never understood what he meant and my parents weren't telling. I don't know if that would help, but there you go."

He looks at Nims and says, "Thank you both. That is important. But what does he mean about the offering bit? Was he referring to you and the girl that he was performing an exorcism on? Are your parents particularly high in standing with the church?"

Lifting my shoulders in a shrug, I tell him, "Not that I noticed. To be honest, while I was a child I went all the time because I had no choice. But the older I got, the less I went. I found reasons not to go as often as I could. I was savagely ill a lot on the weekends. Once I moved out, they still tried to force me to go, but I became adept at pretending I wasn't home. Once I got Nims, I trained her not to bark when people knocked. And to hide. It worked.

We hid and never answered for anyone on a Sunday. I thought it was because of what the other parishioners would think. They worried about that stuff. Now I'm not so sure."

He nods, "We ran a background check on you after you arrived and started coming around the market, but none of these things were available. It helps."

My jaw dropped when he said that. I tell him, "That probably how they found me!"

He flinches before saying, "You might be right. We'll make it up to you, somehow. For now, anything else you can tell us about your parents and the church, especially the church, the better we will be able to figure out why they are after you so hard. And how to stop them without revealing all of our kind to the humans."

I tell him more of what I know about the church, which isn't a whole lot. Mostly impressions filtered through the lens of childhood. The entire time he listens intently, and it's really kind of a turn on. Which reminds me, "I have a date! Shit. I need to get ready."

Duncan frowns, "Are you sure you should be going out right now?"

"No. I'm not. But I am going to. I told Roman that you could come last night, and he okayed it. Maybe it would be a good idea to have another vampire come stay with my dogs, but I am going to go out. I could probably get a couple of the shifters to come stay with them if there aren't any vampires available."

He is scowling now, saying, "That won't be necessary. I'll get someone over and you can introduce them to the dogs. Then you, Nims, and I will go on your date."

I feel a smile growing on my face, "My date. I like the sound of that."

* * *

Getting dressed for my first date in years is more than a little stressful. I want to dress up some, but I don't really own dressy clothing. It's never been a priority for me. I do have some slacks and a nice shirt, I can pair that with heels and put my hair up. I can do this. Deciding to go really light on the makeup, a benefit of being a vampire is gorgeous skin. So liner and mascara, a little tinted gloss, since my hair is going to be up. I grab a clip thing with bead-covered elastic stretching between two clips and use it to secure my hair in a messy updo. Looking in the mirror, I see a stranger. Long brown hair up in clips, green eyes accentuated by liner and mascara, fairly full lips with a bit of shine. A form fitting black shirt emphasizes my hourglass shape, even if it is, as my parents said, a glass too full. The long, dark floral skirt pairs nicely and I think maybe I don't look like a clown, even if I feel like one. Black heels from the back of my closet and I am ready. Heading back downstairs, I hear someone at the door. Duncan is there and answering before I take another step. Blair's voice rings out and I smile, calling down to them, "I'll be right there!" I walk a little faster down the stairs, though I try to avoid seeming too eager by running down like I want to. The dogs, they have no such concern and run to greet him. By the time I get to the doorway, Blair is surrounded by my dogs. They are all eager for his attention. Duncan is off to the side, arms crossed over his chest and looking down at the display with a frown. I have the strangest urge to go comfort him. Shoving that down where I don't have to think about it, I cross over to Blair, "I need to take them outside before we can go. Would you like to walk with me?"

He looks up and his breath catches. He clears his throat and says, "I would very much like that. You look stunning tonight." He stands and I feel almost delicate next to his bulk. It really is the nicest feeling. "Duncan, do you have someone coming to sit with the dogs?"

"Yes, they should be here any time now."

I smile at him and say, "Good, let me know when they arrive."

He grunts as we leave him in the entryway, all the dogs happily following us to the back door. Nims is more dignified than the rest, but she is still obviously happy to see Blair. The dogs don't take long to do their backyard wanderings. Knowing how sensitive Blair's nose is, I am extra grateful for the service that comes by during the day and collects all the poop. The moonlight glints off his dark skin as we wait for the dogs to come. His blue eyes seem to be lit from within. He smells so good; I wonder, is it a cologne or him? He has smelled this good every time I've seen him. The dogs finally finish their business and are heading inside. He gestures for me to go before him. I tell him, "You don't need to be so chivalrous here."

He laughs and says, "It's not chivalry. I wanted to watch your hips swing as you walk."

"Oh!" I shake my head and chuckle, "Well then, who am I to spoil your view?" I feel like I am walking strangely up the stairs and across the porch. I know that if I were still human, I would blush bright red. So, I put my focus on the dogs as they head directly for the front room. It makes walking normally so much easier. In the front room, I find Duncan and two other vampires. He introduces them as Liam and Lauren. The dogs love them and are greeting them happily while Duncan looks rather displeased about the entire thing. "Duncan, are you ready to go? Did you fill Lauren and Liam in on things?"

He nods, "Yes. They know what rooms are off limit and that you value the dogs over everything."

"Excellent! Lauren, Liam, it was very nice to meet you and it looks like my pups approve of you. We'll see you later. If you get hungry, there is food in the kitchen and blood in the basement. Help yourself."

Blair offers an arm after I walk out the door, and it takes me a moment to realize what it is for, because I am still thinking about the way his ass looks in those pants. I've never noticed him from behind, I suppose because he was generally heading towards me as soon as I walked into the store. Slipping my arm through his, we start to walk when I remember the leash in my other hand. "Wait, I need to leash Nims." Freeing my arm from Blair's. I reach down and give her a little petting, touch our foreheads together, and then clip the leash onto her harness. Slipping my arm back into Blair's, I ask him, "So where are we going?"

He smiles, and says in the deep voice of his, "There is a restaurant in the magic sector that serves some of the best food I have ever eaten or smelled. It is called Moments."

I nod, "And they won't mind Nims being with us?"

He says, "No, they are pet friendly. For one, there are too many magical creatures that have fur or feathers or scales. They did work with the witches to get a spell that keeps fur and such out of the food. But once they had that in place, they saw no reason to not allow well-behaved pets in. Your Nims is one of the best behaved pets I have ever seen." Duncan clears his throat behind us and Blair rolls his eyes, saying, "Duncan, I hope you don't think anyone is hiding what Nims is. Everyone except you vampires knows she is..." he looks around before continuing, "different. We are fine with it. And we know the story behind the law the vampires made. The entire rest of the magical world thinks it is the dumbest, most prejudiced law you all have made. It is second only to the one making new vampires slaves for the first five years of their lives."

Duncan snorts and walks faster to be even with us, saying, "They aren't slaves exactly."

Blair growls a little, "And what exactly would you call it?"

Duncan looks away and says, "Perhaps a mentorship?"

A muscle in Blair's cheek dances to a staccato beat and I say, "I think we should change the subject. For the record, I don't know enough about the first five years thing to have an opinion on it. But I would prefer that my first date in over ten years not be marred by my date and my bodyguard fighting."

Blair looks down at me, "What do you mean you don't know about the first five years? Didn't you have to go through that?"

Duncan growls, "Perhaps you shouldn't discuss vampire happenings with shifters?"

Turning my head to look at Duncan, I say, "I will discuss my history and my life with whomever I please. If you don't like it, call Roman and get him to send someone else to act as a bodyguard. You don't get to silence me just because Blair is a shifter and not a vampire." Turning back to Blair, I say, "No, I did not. My turning was, as I understand it, less than conventional. I didn't know that at the time." I tell him the same cliff notes version that I gave Duncan. Blair's eyes move to Nims and back to me, silently asking if I turned her. I tell him, "No, I did not intentionally turn her. We were curled up together when the one that turned me dripped his blood into my mouth. Blood doesn't fall neatly, and it splashes. So Nims was turned by him too. We both woke up the next night, fully healed and craving blood. It was a scary time. Nims handled the craving better than I did. She handled most of it better than I did."

Duncan says, "That's why you both look so sad in the picture, isn't it? It was after you lost everything."

Nims presses her shoulder against my leg and I stroke her head as I say, "Yes, it was. We were homeless then, and the world was not a kind place for us."

Blair says, "I think I would like to talk with your parents. Alone."

Duncan chuckles, "Ah, I would like to join you for that visit."

Blair stops, "I could probably share that visit with you, Duncan. Here we are. Hope you are hungry."

I have been smelling this place for two blocks now. Hungry doesn't cover it.

Twelve

Inside the restaurant, a very nice seeming person with pale green skin and blond hair greets us. Blair informs them he reserved a table and they light up, saying, "Yes, Blair! I recall now. Come, follow me." They lead us through the crowded restaurant to a set of stairs. Up the stairs and to a second floor that is a large, open space surrounded by closed doors. The green person leads us to the third door on the left, opening it and gesturing for us to enter.

We file in and they follow, closing the door. The room is softly lit, with tiny strings of lights everywhere. The table is set to feed four, one chair being specially shaped to accommodate Nims. "Blair, this is amazing. Thank you!"

He smiles down at me, "It's an unconventional date, but I still wanted it to be special. What better way to do that than to make Nims feel included?"

Lifting onto my toes, I throw my arms around him and hug him. He makes this wonderful rumbling noise in his chest as his arms come round me. Duncan clears his throat and I remember it isn't just Nims here. The person asks us to please be seated, saying, "Your server will be here shortly. Their name is Joy. May I send them with drinks?"

Blair asks, "Do you like red wine?"

"Yes, I do."

He turns to the green host person, "We'd like three glasses of red, and a dish of water, please."

"I'll get that sent to you straightaway. Enjoy your evening."

Once they have left the room, I ask Blair, "Is there a library or bookstore somewhere that I can gain more knowledge about the different magical peoples? A website? I want to become more knowledgeable because I am seeing that I know so little."

"Most of us grow up being taught about the magical world, and vampires are generally taught by their maker, but I guess that didn't happen here. I would try Lydia's bookstore. She is one of the witches. I feel certain that she would be more than happy to help you. If there is a book or books that would teach you, she'll have them or be able to get them."

"Oh good! Maybe I can visit her store tomorrow."

Duncan chimes in, "You probably shouldn't go out so much while you are being hunted."

Glaring at him, I start to tell him where he can stick his ideas when Blair says, "Why don't we go tonight? It isn't far from here and right now you have two of us here to guard you. Seems like an opportunity too good to pass up."

I smile widely at him, "That would be wonderful! You really don't mind taking me there?"

He smiles, "I would take you anywhere you asked just so I could be in your presence."

Duncan snorts, but I feel all kinds of happy that someone wants to spend their time in my company. Before I can speak, our server walks in with our wine. This person looks mostly human, but that could be an illusion. They drop off our drinks and recite to us what is available. I don't recognize any of it. I guess my face told everyone that because they discussed it among themselves and our server left shortly after. Thankfully, they also decided for Nims.

"So, um, what did you order for us?"

Blair grins, "For Nims, we ordered what you would consider an exotic steak. It's from an animal that is a huge nuisance, both to the magical community and the humans alike."

Duncan says, "The magical community spends a fair amount of time hunting them because they are running through human areas fucking things up. We didn't want to let it go to waste. It's a lot of good meat, so now when they are hunted down, they go into a butcher shop and we get food. It has been working for a long time. Long enough that people aren't seeing them so damn much now. The deaths have really dropped since we implemented the program."

"What is that much of a nuisance? Is it worldwide? Would I have seen one?"

Blair says, "Seen is really not quite the right word for it. My understanding is that humans don't really see them completely. The ones that can see it, it appears more like an apparition of sorts. They love playing in traffic, causing slow downs and massive wrecks. They feed on the death."

I can't believe these creatures have gone unnoticed for so long by humans. I tell them, "What are they, exactly?

What do you call them? Do humans have a name for them?"

Duncan looks away, tugging at his collar. Blair grimaces, "They do actually. I believe humans call them unicorns."

"What?" I cannot have heard that correctly. There is no way he said unicorns. Putting a finger in my ear and jiggling it a bit to dislodge whatever has my hearing so off, once I remove the finger, I look at Blair. He still looks very serious. "I don't think I heard you correctly. Did you say unicorns?"

He nods, saying, "I did."

"What? Unicorns? Pretty horses with magical horns that love innocence and light?"

He shrugs, saying, "Well, they are pretty. The horns absorb death energy and help them stay unseen. Admittedly, they rarely kill innocent women and children wandering about and they have let themselves be seen in the company of such occasionally. They are really just violent little murder muffins with attached stabbers."

"Holy shit. Everything I know about them is completely wrong."

Our server enters the room then, carrying a folding stand while a large tray of food floats along behind them. I watch as they set out the folding stand, and the tray comes to rest gently on it. I still do not know what they got me to eat. Nims plate floats past me to land gently on the table before her. Her unicorn steak is cut into large chunks stacked prettily on the plate. I can't help but imagine the meat sparkling with magic the way I pictured unicorns before tonight. I realize that my plate is in front of me, so I turn and thank our server. They are gracious and ask if we need anything more. Blair shakes his head, saying, "No, I think we are good for now. Thank you."

As soon as the server clears the door, I ask, "What am I eating?"

Blair chuckles, saying, "Salmon. Look at your plate. It's just plain salmon."

Duncan is trying not to laugh and failing as I look at my plate, entirely relieved to see plain old salmon and not anything that I grew up drawing in pretty little pictures. Nims has no such concerns about unicorn meat. She is eating and looks thoroughly pleased. I guess stabby death horse tastes great.

Ok, I need to focus on my date. That is just a very raw steak there. I pick up my fork and dig in. Chewing slowly, I am straining my brain to figure out something to talk about that isn't unicorns. But how do I get unicorn cows out of my head?

Blair clears his throat, then asks, "Are you enjoying your salmon?"

Swallowing, I say, "Yes, it is very good. What are you having?"

He smirks like he knows I have concerns for more unicorn steak, saying, "It is a plain steak. Was once a cow."

Duncan snorts, saying, "In case anyone is interested, I am having ostrich. It is entirely tasty, unlike this date, which is incredibly boring and a little sad."

"Shut up, Duncan. Nobody asked you. Blair, how was your day? Anything interesting happen?"

Blair grins and launches into a story about a leprechaun and a witch with a Saint Bernard. We laugh our way through dinner. Duncan is steadily growing more sour throughout but I don't care. Blair is fantastic as he leads Nims and me back through the restaurant and down the street. He stops us in front of a green building. There are no windows, and the door is red. There are no signs, and I don't think I have ever seen a brick building that shade of green. Looking up at him, I say, "I thought we were going to a bookstore?"

He laughs, "This is it."

"This is the bookstore? How do you know if it's open? Why aren't there any windows? A sign? How does anyone know this is a bookstore?"

Blair laughs, "Most of us grew up here. Someone took us here. So now I am bringing you here. And you will know where it is and when it is open. You won't be without books on magical things and you won't be relying on the human library."

"Well, okay then. Take me, sir, I'm ready for the grand bookstore."

He laughs and slips my arm into the crook of his, opens the door and leads me into sheer magnificence. It looked so small on the outside. But inside, the building soars in magnificence. I can't begin to guess how they got all this into what looked like such a small building from the outside.

The ceilings are so high up I am unsure of the color. Shelves line the walls and fill the space, books and strange things overflowing them. Chandeliers are hanging at intervals, but I can't quite tell what they are made of. They seem to move. I am completely entranced as I wander the aisles created by the shelves. I find books on magical animals, magic, vampire society. Holy shit, vampire society.

Suddenly, I realize morning is nearly here. Nims is still by my side, but I don't see anyone else. I have an armful of books and I don't know where I am. "Well, Nims, let's see if we can find the checkout and maybe get ourselves home before the sun comes up."

Nims turns and starts down the aisle. I follow her because she was probably paying attention. She leads me directly to the checkout. There is a tiny person standing on a stool watching us approach. As I set the books down, the person says, "You're new. My name isn't pronounceable with a human tongue. You may call me Rose. You have books for learning. Did you not grow up in the magical community? Were you not trained? Are you a researcher? Do you read fiction? Did you find all the aisles? Do you live close enough to make it home before the sunrise?"

Feeling a little stunned by the rapid speech, I say, "I, uh, thank you, Rose. I was not trained, nor did I grow up in the magical community. I research for the books I write, but these books are for me to learn. So I don't offend anyone. I live close enough to make it home by sunrise as long as I checkout fairly fast."

Rose nods, "Your total is seventy-five eighty-nine. I will see you again soon. The door will open for you. I expect you will bring the dog too. She is very well behaved."

Handing over the money, I tell her, "She is. She's my best friend. I don't know what I would do without her."

She nods, "It shows. Go. You need to get home."

Collecting my books, I tell her, "Thanks Rose. I can't wait to come back here. Say, I had a couple of people with me when I came in. You wouldn't happen to know where they are? I seem to have lost them."

She smiles, the creases of her face folding to make her even more lovely. She says, "They are near the door. The seats are there for the waiting ones. Blair has already gotten books this week and Duncan frowns heavily in his presence tonight. It has been entertaining. Have a lovely day!"

"I will. Thank you again."

She nods and disappears, not even a puff of smoke to mark her leaving. This place is so cool. We head for the door and find the two of them sitting exactly where Rose said they would be. Blair smiles and stands, "May I carry your books for you?"

"Yes, you may." Duncan is still quite frown-ish as he stands and walks to the door.

The walk home is fast, because while I won't immediately burn anymore for being exposed to the sunlight, it doesn't take long. Once we arrive, I ask Blair if he would like to come in and have a drink before he goes.

He smiles ruefully and gestures at the window where Duncan is glowering out at us, saying, "Perhaps a different night, after Duncan gets himself sorted. He has a hell of a crush on you."

My jaw falls open, "What? No way. He is a jerk to me on a regular basis. No way is he crushing on me. Even if he were in some weird, alternate universe, does that mean that we aren't going to go out again? Or that I am not getting a good morning kiss?"

He pulls me into his arms, saying, "No, it simply means I am going to give you time to read your new books today. And you are definitely getting a good morning kiss." He lowers his lips to mine as my arms slide up around his neck. It's an explosion when our lips touch, fire racing through my veins as his arms tighten around me, lifting me off the ground. I hear a sound, but it is so far away and I really don't care until Blair breaks the kiss. Both of us are breathing heavily as I realize Nims is growling low in her throat. Turning glazed feeling eyes in her direction, I see she is growling at the house.

Blair chuckles, saying, "Our audience doesn't appreciate the show and Nims doesn't appreciate the audience. He should take care. She isn't above biting his ass. She knows he will heal."

A giggle rises unbidden, the image of Nims biting Duncan in the ass thoroughly entertaining. Blair smiles down at me as he releases me and I tell him, "I really enjoyed the night. You should come over soon. Let me cook for you."

Blair nods, "I would love that. When would you like me over?"

"Tomorrow sounds about right to me?"

His smile is so wide I wonder if he will hurt himself as he says, "I can't wait, around midnight?"

"Perfect. I'll see you then."

He leans in and kisses my forehead, then tips my face up with a finger under my chin to kiss my lips. The kiss is sweet, but I can still feel the fire inside leaping up, until it is stifled by the sound of Duncan rapping on the window frame. The audacity on that man.

Thirteen

As soon as Blair disappears from sight, Nims and I go in the house. Greeting all the dogs after they sit and completely ignoring Duncan. We head for the kitchen after the greetings. I know the puppies are hungry. I generally feed them well before sunrise. All the bowls out and lined up, I have the assembly line going as I talk to Nims, telling her, "I know this will not be the easiest thing for either of us. And I know that most of the aggravation is going to fall on you and I am so sorry for that. The witches and the shifters don't care, but the vampires really care. Kind of says something about the way the witches and shifters accept you for who you have proven to be, while the vampires would have you dead just because of what you are, doesn't it?"

She woofs gently at me in agreement and then Duncan walks in the kitchen saying, "That's a little harsh, don't you think?"

Looking him in the eye, I say, "No more harsh than the fact that the vampire world we were thrust into with no choice in the matter would murder her simply for existing. Not because she has done anything wrong, just because she exists. I feel like that is pretty fucking harsh. But I guess you think it's just part of the vampire society and something that we all need to learn to live with." I drag in a breath, shouting, "But it's crap! Becoming vampires might have saved us, but what good will it have done if it just meant we would be killed later by the vampires? Because if she dies, so will I. There is no me without her. And honestly, right now I like the witches and the shifters better!"

Duncan nods, "I understand. Perhaps you could convince Nims that I am not a threat to you?"

I look down and see that Nims is standing directly in front of me, facing him. She is silent as a tomb but the fur along her back is raised and her body is tensed to attack, "Nims, sweetheart," she looks back at me and her whole body relaxes, "he isn't an actual danger. I'm yelling at him because I am angry, not for danger." She nods and sits right where she is, facing Duncan.

He chuckles, "Not a threat, but not trusted. That's fair, I suppose."

"Not trusted is what you get," I tell him as I turn back to getting the dogs' bowls ready, "when you butt into other people's conversations. You should be glad I haven't bitten you! God knows, you deserve it!" Grabbing up a couple of bowls and starting the process of setting them in their holders. Every one of the dogs is sitting and waiting patiently while I set the bowls in place. Stepping back after setting the last bowl in place, I tell the dogs, "Enjoy, puppies."

Duncan clears his throat, "I actually came in here for a

reason. Roman wants to see us. He wants us to come to his home as soon as it is dark out."

"Why?"

"He said there are complications, and he needs to know more."

Sitting at the table, I ask him, "Is it going to take very long? I have a date tomorrow."

He scowls, growling out, "I have better things to do than to follow you about on dates."

Raising my brows at his tone, I tell him, "Well, that's unfortunate. Guess we will have to do without your sparkling company. However shall we survive the loss?"

His brows drop and he leans forward, saying, "I am your bodyguard until this thing is over. You aren't going anywhere without me."

Smiling sweetly, I tell him, "Guess you are going on a date with us." Nims sits next to me and I extend a hand to scratch behind her ears, "Just because this situation coincided with Blair and me starting to date doesn't mean I am going to put it off. It isn't like he is taking me out to wander Inverness. He is collecting me and taking me to the magic sector. A place that they can't go. I am technically safer in there than I am at my home with you. That's it! Why don't you go do whatever you need to do while we have our date inside the magical sector? It would give you time off, and I would get to have a date without the grumpy chaperone. It's a win-win deal."

I can't help but think he should do something about that anger problem he has as he grits out, "Thank you for the consideration but until Roman says otherwise, I will stay by your side at all times. Even through boring and unimaginative dates."

"Excuse you! That date was not at all boring or unimaginative. He took me to a place that I had never been before. He was really nice to you even though you were rude most of the evening, and then he took me to a magical bookstore. That date was perfect with the glaring exception of your presence!"

He raises a brow as if he doesn't believe me, saying, "It would appear that the dogs are finished eating. You should get some sleep. Night will be here before you know it."

"Gee, thanks Dad. This is what I have been missing for the past twenty years. Some man to tell me when I should get some sleep. Thank you!"

"That's not what I meant."

Holding up my hand at him, I tell him, "Stop. I don't want to hear it. I am taking my dogs outside, letting them do their business, and then I am going to bed."

He looks terrified, saying, "You can't go outside! The sunlight will kill you!"

My eyes roll without my intending to as I say, "Thanks for the newsflash. Super helpful. Here's one for you. I have a porch and I don't have to go out into the sun. It is shaded, no direct sunlight. Perhaps today has been too much for you in your advanced age. Maybe you should get some sleep."

He stands, growls at me, then turns on his heel and leaves the kitchen.

* * *

She is doing this on purpose. There is no way it always takes her this long to feed the dogs and let them do their business. She's still in her pajamas, for fuck's sake! We need to get to Roman's house before he sends people out to find us. I head for the porch and as soon as I step out the door; I see all the damn dogs sitting on the porch while she reads a damn paper. Why? Why did Roman assign me here? "Olivia." She completely ignores me so I say, "Olivia, if you don't get moving so we can get out of here and get to Roman's house, I will pick you up and take you there in your pajamas. None of us is going to be bothered by it, but we should have been there already and Roman is going to send people to search for us soon if you don't get moving."

She looks up from her paper, asking, "Do you have someone here to stay with the dogs?"

"Yes! They got here twenty minutes ago! They are even willing to deal with Nims condescension. Now can we get going?"

She looks confused, "What do you mean deal with Nims? She isn't staying here. Nims goes where I go. If Roman doesn't like that, he can drag himself down here."

"Fine! But she is going to have to act like a dog! That means a leash on her. She can't look at anyone like their intelligence is being questioned, even if we are all thinking it. Do you understand that not even the witches will be able to protect her if this is widely known?"

Ah, fuck. Now she looks mad as she stands. She's so cute, glaring up at me like that. Fuck, no! Not cute! She is just an assignment, nothing more. What the hell is wrong with me? She stomps over to stand directly in front of me and says, "Perhaps if your old ass can't even remember the conversation you eavesdropped on last night, you should take a break. Maybe Roman could send someone else to take your place, that can keep two thoughts in their mind at one time. Or does he just set his standards that low? Should I ask him? You know, it doesn't matter. I am going to ask him about his standards. We know how Nims needs to act. The only one in this room that doesn't seem able to act as they should is you! We will be ready to go shortly."

She sails around me and all the dogs follow her in. Nims glares at me till the last dog passes before she follows as well, snorting at me when she passes me.

Great. The dog is disgusted with me. Just fucking fabulous. Less than ten minutes later, she is back downstairs, ready to go.

Opening the door, I wait for her to walk through. She walks directly toward the door till the last minute when she turns into the room where two vampires are sitting with the dogs. Dammit! "Olivia, we need to go!"

She says, in this grating, singsong voice, "Not until I have said goodbye to all my dogs."

Interminable minutes later, she finally comes out and walks thru the door. Finally. As we are walking, she asks, "Why aren't we going toward the market?"

With a sigh, I tell her, "Because Roman doesn't live at the market. He does business there. And since you couldn't get out of the house on time, he will probably be late for his meetings tonight."

She snorts, "Then he should set meetings with me by calling me or messaging me. As I was not included in the meeting's planning, you all can deal with it. If you want me to be more cordial, you all should try it."

A growl erupts out of me, and I say, "Fine. I'll make sure Roman gets in touch with you about it from now on. Fucking hell, he didn't have your number. Neither did I."

She rattles off her number, and I plug it into my phone, immediately sharing it with Roman. The rest of the walk to Roman's is silent. As we get close to the gate, I pull the leash out of my pocket and hold it out to Olivia. She stares at it for a moment before taking it from my hand. I stop with her as she apologizes to Nims and clips the leash to her collar. Nims doesn't seem to hold it against Olivia. Nope. It's me she glares at. That dog is going to bite me one day. At the gate, I swing it open and let them walk through before me. They stop before going too far, staring up at the house. I forget how grand a structure it is. We've been here so long. The advent of modern society and large, impersonal cities has meant that we don't have so much need to move around. The house was built for Roman. He was one of the dastardly English bastards taking over Scottish lands. Though he did his part to make up for it by feeding only on the English Lords for a hundred years or so. He jokes occasionally that he has royal blood by infusion now. The old place is pretty grand. The fountain blocks a fair part of the view of the front entrance, though. So I tell them, "Come, it's more impressive on the other side of the fountain." Olivia and Nims begin moving again. I lead them, telling them little bits of the history of this place. Olivia is entranced with the place, though she is listening intently to every word about the history of it as well.

She stops in front of the door, saying, "Wow, he really went all out with the carvings here. It isn't often you find a door surrounded by such beautiful workmanship. What are the creatures in the carvings? Imaginary or magical?"

"Both," I say, "They included both so that when humans see it, they think it is all imaginary creatures. He even included unicorns. Roman created this. He studied the art of carving for some time and became superb at it. He only does a piece occasionally now, but his skill is unparalleled. Come, let's get in and get this over with. Roman is waiting for us." She nods and we walk to the door, but before I can get to it, it swings open to reveal Niall.

He greets us, saying, "Hello, so glad you have made it. Roman was considering sending someone out for you until I saw you both admiring the edifice. He was rather pleased about that and allowed that he would wait until you had a good, long look. So, have you finished your look or do you need a few more minutes, gorgeous?"

Olivia smiles at him like he is her favorite person in the world. I don't like it. Moving to stand directly in his line of sight to her, I ask, "Where is Roman?"

Niall grins at me, saying, "His office, of course. Have you really been gone long enough already to forget his routine?"

He walks around me and offers his arm to Olivia, saying, "Here, take my arm and I shall take you, milady." he grins at her suggestively and I like that even less. Then he continues, "To Roman's office, where this meeting will take place. Before we go, may I be introduced to your faithful companion?"

She looks flattered as she introduces Nims to him. What the hell is wrong with Niall? And why does the damn dog like him? He shouldn't be flirting with her like this. She's here to see Roman. Clearing my throat, I say, "Excuse me, if we are finished with introductions and whatever nonsense you are pulling Niall, perhaps we could get to the reason we are here?"

Niall grins at me before turning back to her, saying, "Olivia, allow me to take you to Roman."

I follow behind them until an ungodly odor assaults my nostrils. It feels like my nose is burning. I look up just in time to see Nims looking entirely too satisfied as she turns the corner down the hall. Dammit! She farted down the hall on purpose! Why does that fucking dog hate me so much?

Fourteen

O livia

Duncan is jealous. I don't get it. Niall is perfectly charming and completely uninterested in me. He is the nicest vampire I have met so far, and I think I want him to be my friend. No. No friends. That is never a good idea. They just turn on you later. Niall is telling me about the house, which is more like a palace, as he guides me through the maze of hallways. Apparently, there are several famous people in the paintings lining the walls. Most of the paintings were done by artists that are very important to history. He points to a room, saying, "This is his Egyptian room. Roman keeps the things he gained from different tombs and times in there. He also has quite the collection of African pieces along with a vast collection of Indigenous items he has collected over the years."

My brain screeches to a halt. He can't mean what I think he means. "What do you mean by collected?"

Niall says, "Oh, well, he has been alive for a very long time. He took part in a great many history-making events.

There are spoils of war, things he collected on expeditions, he acquired it all in various ways. Here we are." He stops us and raps smartly on the door to the right.

I hear Roman tell us to come in, and I can't wait to give him a piece of my mind. He stands and smiles on the other side of the desk, faltering when he sees my face, and frowning as I say, "How long have you been stealing from other cultures? Why do you think that is all right? What is wrong with you?"

He is still frowning as he says, "I collected those pieces fairly as part of war or exploration. Sometimes both. They are mine to do with as I please."

"Fucking amazing. Live for hundreds of years, still have the self awareness of a rock. What you were doing was stealing from people. Why haven't you given it back?"

He runs a hand over his face. With a deep sigh, he says, "If I promise to look into what the hell you are talking about and give it due consideration, can we move on?"

Glaring at him, I ask, "And will you tell me the results of your research? Will we speak about it further at a future date?"

"Yes, we will. Only if you will drop it for now. I want to at least know why you are yelling at me about my collection so I can formulate a proper argument. Today, we have bigger things to concern ourselves with. Things like keeping you alive so the witches don't wipe us out. What did you do to make them like you so much?"

I shrug, saying, "I don't know. Maybe it's Nims. She really is the best dog and my best friend."

Roman raises a brow and I kneel next to Nims, putting an arm around her. She is grinning her beautiful, goofy grin. A little string of drool is falling onto Roman's expensive carpet. Whoops. When I look up at Roman, he doesn't look terribly impressed. Well, he is obviously not that smart a man, anyway. Giving Nims a squeeze, I stand up again. Roman says, "Whatever may have done it, they are serious. If you die, we all do. And that means that you are incredibly important to all of us."

At this point, Duncan steps forward and starts talking to him. They talk about all the things I told him and both of them are ignoring us. Niall nudges my elbow with his and says, "Would you like to tour the grounds?"

A smile growing on my face, I tell him I would love that. Duncan glares at me and I say, "I would greatly prefer to have a walk with someone pleasant to be around while you discuss my life as though I am not here, anyway."

Duncan snarls and starts around the desk toward me. Roman snaps, "Duncan!" He stops mid-step and turns back to Roman, who waves us to go on. Probably relieved to not worry about me berating him for all his stolen goods.

Niall is so smug looking as he guides me out of the room. Nims is near bouncing with happiness as we go. After we get down the hall a bit, I say, "Just checking here. You aren't interested in me that way, are you?"

He laughs, "Sorry love, you don't have the parts I prefer."

I am laughing as I say, "Duncan has no idea, does he?"

Niall shakes his head no, saying, "Nah, I'm new here, and he hasn't paid any attention to who I am interested in as a partner."

"Well, I think you and I could be great friends. Plus, his

ridiculous behavior can entertain us till he realizes you would be interested in him way more than you would ever be in me."

He has this adorable smirk on his face as he says, "Well, you will be my very first vampire friend and we will have the best time."

"First? How is that possible?"

He shrugs, "I haven't been turned very long. I am still in my first five years of service."

Tipping my head to one side, I ask, "Five years of service? What is that?"

He explains, and I am floored. I think I might have dodged a bullet by sheer fucking luck. He finishes and says, "Did you not do five years of service after you were turned?"

I shrug, saying, "No. I didn't even know his name. And I never saw him again after that night. He said he would come back, but I never saw him."

Niall frowns and stops walking. Turning to face me, he says, "I've never heard of anything like that. Did you even consent to being turned?"

I laugh, but he looks very serious as I tell him, "No. I didn't even know what was happening at first."

He pulls me into a hug, rubbing my back as he says, "Oh love, I am so sorry! That must have been terrifying for you! You are so strong to have gotten through it all on your own." He leans away, his hands going to my arms as he looks into my eyes. He says, "Any time you need to talk about it, or anything else, I am here for you." Then his arms are pulling me back into a hug and it feels like a stitch pops in my chest. My eyes are feeling a little misty as Nims presses into the two of us.

It is a beautiful moment ruined by Duncan saying, "It's barely been ten minutes. What the fuck are you doing in his arms?"

Nims snorts at him, and I step back as Niall releases me. Wiping at my eyes while I am still facing away from him, I say, "Pretty sure that's none of your business." Niall grins at me and gives me a surreptitious thumbs up so I know I am safe to turn around without him seeing my tears.

Duncan says, "We are finished inside. You should come back in now. Before another enforcer somehow ends up with you in his arms."

Nims has on her regal airs as she walks past Duncan with us following, giggling as his scowl grows deeper. I can't resist and as we walk by I tell him, "You know, I was always told that if you make faces like that a lot your face will freeze like that." Niall loses it at that point and leans against a wall as he laughs. I grab his arm, "Come on, before Dad takes a switch to both our bottoms." He is gasping with laughter as we stagger back into the house.

Duncan

Following them through the house is just annoying. How are they so close in this short amount of time? Staggering into the house like they are drunk. Disgraceful. Niall has pulled himself together, but they are still walking arm in arm.

Niall asks her, "Is Nims your only dogs or do you have more?"

She tells him about the others and invites him to visit and meet the other dogs. This is ridiculous. I ask her, "Should you really be inviting people to your house when there are other people trying to kill you through exorcism?"

She looks back at me, raises a brow and says, "Are you saying you don't trust your family?"

Niall stops and turns to face me, "Is that what you are saying, Duncan? Am I someone you don't trust?"

I wonder if it hurts to grow back teeth. I think mine are going to break from the pressure of my jaw clenching. Tipping my head from side to side to pop my neck, I say, "Niall, I trust you just fine. Right now, I am pretty sure you are just trying to get into her pants."

The two of them are laughing again as they turn and walk towards Roman's office. I can hear Niall whispering to her, "I didn't think it would start so quickly! You haven't even..."

She shakes her head no, whispering back, "Nothing. Nothing at all."

Roman would be annoyed if I picked the two of them up and shake some sense into them. I know he would. But the temptation is really strong right now. Following them into the office, I watch as they sit in the two chairs at the front of Roman's desk. I move to stand behind the two of them, right in the middle, so I can keep an eye on both of them.

Roman raises a brow at me then looks to Olivia, saying, "Your parents look like fine, upstanding people, with one exception. They have no jobs. The only money they have appears to come from the church. Why would they be getting money from the church?"

Olivia's hand goes to her chest, "I don't know. I thought my father had a job. As far as I knew, he went to work every day. What was he doing?"

Roman shrugs, "I can't answer that. According to the background check, he hasn't worked since you were born. Your mother hasn't either. Even the house they live in is owned by the church."

"What? I don't understand? Why would the church give them a house? What does this mean?"

Roman tells her he doesn't know and then asks, "Did you know your parent's church has offices in every country?"

"What? They're just a Southern Baptist church. There's one on every corner in the southern US. Why would they need an office in every country?"

He says, "I don't know, but they are owned by a corporation. Southich. S-o-u-t-h-i-c-h. Any idea what those letters stand for?"

"I thought it was just the name of the church?"

Roman nods, "I thought that at first, but this looks like they stand for something. We are going to continue to investigate this. Maybe learning more about your parent's connection to the church will shed some light on why the church is so determined to hunt you. In the meantime, Duncan is going to continue to stay with you. Niall, if you repeat the rest of this anywhere, I'll kill you myself. Whatever you do, don't let any other vampire close to Nims. If they realize what she is, we will all be in a world of trouble."

Olivia nods, "I know. We are going to work at making

sure no other vampires notice her true nature. It won't be the easiest thing for my super smart girl. Playing dumb isn't her thing." Nims whimpers right then, the big ham. Olivia continues, "I think I need to get her home. We rarely spend so much time outside the house and away from the other dogs."

Fifteen

Olivia

The walk home seemed like an eternity. Duncan is still pissy about Niall. Niall thinks it is hilarious and made sure to put his number into my phone before we left. I thought he might choke on the laughter he was holding back as Duncan fumed in silence. We did make it back to my beautiful little home. The dogs were happy to see us as we were gone for most of the night. The two vampires that sat with the dogs were lovely and left their card, saying that this is the best assignment ever and they would love to come back again. I thanked them and told them I would call them soon. Now, I am working on getting the dogs fed and Duncan is at the table. Watching. In silence. I could tell him that Niall prefers men, but this is a lot more fun since he cannot retaliate against Niall. I freeze as the sound of breaking glass reaches me.

I start to turn to Duncan when the glass in the kitchen door breaks and all hell explodes in my kitchen. "Nims! Get the dogs downstairs," I shout as I sling a food dish like a frisbee at the arm trying to unlock the door. She lets loose a howl that cuts through all the barking. The dogs run down the stairs to the basement, where they will be safe. I keep throwing dog dishes at intruders. I hear a ringing noise and I realize Duncan left his phone on the table after he started a call. Duncan is fighting two men, I manage to get one in the head with a dish. Someone says hello over the phone and Duncan yells, "We are under attack!"

The voice on the phone says we're coming right as someone grabs my arm. Swinging around, I nail him in the face with my other hand and, grabbing the front of his pants, toss him at the wall. Nims gets up the stairs about then and leaps at the man before he can recover.

I turn to face the door, and a man's fist hits me in the face. "Fuck!" I shout as I shove him away with both hands. My eyes open just in time to see him hit the open door, smashing it to bits. More men are pouring into my kitchen. I can hear Nims fighting, and there are three men coming at me. I kick one and hit another, but the third stabs me in my side with one of those fucking silver crosses. More men are surrounding me, stabbing me. It seems like for every one that I knock down, two more replace him. Nims howls in rage, and Duncan is shouting something, but I can't tell what over the men around me yelling, "Die demon, die." Suddenly, men fly away and I can keep them at bay a little better. I've lost too much blood. I'm slow and weak. Then Nims is next to me. She rips a man's arm off and uses it to beat some others. More just keep coming and I am getting slower. I can't let them see what I am. What if they escape? I have to keep them from hurting Nims.

* * *

Duncan

Too many! Too many motherfuckers in this damned tiny ass kitchen! At least Nims got to her. She is side by side fighting with Olivia. If I can get rid of a few more of these assholes, I can take some of the pressure off them.

Just then I hear feet pounding the pavement. Fuck, if that isn't Roman, we are done. There must be twenty religious nut jobs here in the kitchen. Then I see the men crowding the hall take flight. They're here! Even as the relief sets in, I see one attacker with a pile of paper trying to start a fire. Before I can do anything, there is a loud pop, and two witches are standing behind the guy with the fire. Man, is he screwed. The witches get real fuckin' touchy about fire. He is the first one they zap. He falls over and the witches just keep zapping everyone that isn't a vampire.

Olivia is faltering, and the hunger takes over. She grabs one man and feeds. His struggles avail him nothing as she drains him. Nims is shaking another man like a toy. As Olivia drops the man she fed from, another one lying on the floor tries to stab her. The men I was fighting are all out, frozen by the witches. Olivia snatches up the man that tried stabbing her and tells him, "I'm real fucking tired of being stabbed." She punches him in the face before dropping him to the ground and kicking the hell out of him. If I'm not mistaken, the wet crunching sound he made means that some of his ribs are residing in his lungs now. I watch her as she looks around, realizing that the threat is over. She is covered in blood, most of it hers. She sinks down next to

Nims and wraps an arm around her. Nims leans into her. They lean their heads against each other and just sit there. I don't think I have ever seen two people as close as that woman and her dog. We can't let anyone take that dog from her, no matter what.

Sixteen

Olivia

Nims is ok. I just keep telling myself that for a moment as I keep my face next to hers. I was so afraid I would lose her. Opening my eyes and I see the witches smiling down at us, Niall looking terrified as he looks at Nims. The two other vampires behind him are looking at us with suspicion in their eyes. Niall meets my eyes and gives me the slightest nod. Then he spins around to face Roman, putting himself between us, "We can't kill the dog. I don't care about any laws. That dog was not frenzied. She was fighting to save her person."

One witch chimes in, "We agree. And as we have already said, the dog lives."

Roman scowls at them, "This isn't your call."

The witches laugh and one says, "If the woman or the dog dies, we will consider it an act of war. They are under our protection. We have let you handle this only so that you would not lose face in your world. We can rid this region of every vampire in it, and we will, if anything happens to end their lives."

Roman's scowl grows deeper as he says, "Why? What is so special about this one girl and her dog?"

The witches laugh again, "You'll know in the fullness of time. Keep them alive." With that pronouncement, they disappear, only a loud pop to mark their travel.

Roman is rubbing his forehead with one hand while all the vampires are standing still, waiting to see what he decides. Nims and I are as good as dead if he decides war with the witches is worth it so long as we are dead. I want to ease myself in front of her, but I suspect he would notice and take offense. He drops his hand and meets my eyes, "You are getting adopted into this family. There is not a chance in hell we are going through this much fucking trouble and you will not be part of our family. You are ten years into being a vampire and seem to have done reasonably well, considering the lack of training. Not to mention you have valuable allies in the witches. Having the dog is a liability," his eyes narrow as my arm tightens around Nims, "but we can slowly work to get the law changed. Will you consent to joining our family?"

I am breathing a little easier, but I don't trust this. They only wanted to help me because Ailsa told them to, and I don't know what it means to be part of their family. If I would be under control all the time like his enforcers are, I want no part of that. "I need to know more about what this will mean for me. We don't want to be at anyone's beck and call. I have a life, a job."

Roman nods, "That's fair." He looks around at the

vampires that came with him, "You all understand the need to keep this quiet, correct?" They nod, their faces still a little pinched and fearful. Roman says, "I can vouch for the dog at this point. She has been turned as long as Olivia and we have had her as a guest at the estate. The only vampire she seems to have any disagreement with is Duncan, whom she seems to believe is dumb." The vampires snicker and relax. Maybe Roman isn't entirely a pain. "Olivia," he says as he turns back to me, "I think, considering the state of your home right now, perhaps you should come stay at my house for a time. The security is much higher there, and they sent numbers to overwhelm you tonight. Plus, cleanup is going to be a while here. This is a fair number of bodies. And pieces."

"And my dogs are invited too, right?"

Roman looks back at me, "Yes, I told you Nims is fine at the house."

Chuckling, I say, "No, my dogs. With an s. I have more dogs. Nims took them down to the basement when the attack started. I can't leave them here alone. They would be heartbroken."

Roman sighs, "How many dogs, precisely?"

"Fifteen. Plus Nims."

"What the fuck do you need with fifteen damn dogs?"

"Well, I like dogs. They are way better company and they never ask me dumb questions or say that I don't need another dog, they just love. But, I actually foster them and find them new homes. There are a couple that are permanent because people are the worst and they can't be persuaded to trust a human again. So far, they all are fine with vampires and shifters. Especially shifters."

"Fine, yes, the dogs too. Bring the fucking dogs. Pack to

stay for a bit. I would like for you to stay until we can up the security here as well."

"I'm not sure I like the idea of upped security here, but I guess I can live with it. But you know the dogs all stay inside with me, right?" I take my arm off Nims and stand as I tell her, "Go get the others, please."

Roman nods, "It couldn't possibly be any other way, could it?"

I can't help but grin as I say, "No, it really couldn't. But here they are now. Look how well behaved they are."

Roman glares at me and at the dogs as they enter the bloodbath that is my kitchen. He looks at their feet in the blood and says, "Make sure you clean their feet before you bring them into my house." I have the most awful urge to giggle, but I swallow it down as he tells Niall and Duncan, "The two of you help her get whatever she needs to the house. Make sure those fucking dogs' feet are clean and dry before they step inside. And don't fucking lose any of them. God only knows the witches might start a war over some bedraggled ass chihuahua." He leaves, his two vampires following him, without so much as a goodbye. I'm sure he has visions of dog prints all over his ancient and expensive rugs dancing through his head. Niall has already waded into the middle of the dogs and is currently trying to pet them all at the same time.

I guess I need to pack. "Duncan, can you help me find the dishes for their food? I still have to feed them."

He laughs, "It surprised me when the first dish flew past my head."

I laugh too, "Yes, I was surprised by that as well. My aim was way off with that one. I was aiming for a different guy entirely. I thought it was going to hit you." The look of shock on his face is the best as I turn toward the kitchen door to try to find any of the dishes I threw in that direction.

* * *

I am getting things ready when I hear Blair at the front door. All the dogs race to greet him, while Nims and I take a more sedate pace. When I get to the entry, I can see he is petting all the dogs, but worry is etched into his face as he takes in my appearance. He straightens and comes to stand in front of me, "Olivia, what happened? Are you okay? Why were you bleeding so much?"

He grasps my shoulders with his powerful hands and turns me around, thoroughly inspecting my body. When I am facing him again, I tell him, "They attacked my house. Well, me. They attacked me here, in my house. I think I need to cancel our date tonight. My kitchen has seen better days. They have a clean-up crew coming, but I still have to get things repaired."

Blair shakes his head, "You aren't staying here tonight, right? Do you need a place to stay? You and all the dogs can come to my place."

"I really appreciate that, but Roman has already decided that we are going to his home. I'm not really sure he will take no for an answer, what with the witches telling him to protect me."

His brows creep up as he says, "The witches were here tonight?"

"They were. It was a fairly large attack. Big enough that

they would have overwhelmed us if Roman and the witches hadn't got here when they did."

"Why didn't anyone call me?"

With a shrug, I tell him, "I don't have your phone number and I think Duncan has to call Roman. I don't know if someone called the witches or they just showed up."

He frowns, "Where is your phone?"

I check my back pockets, because there are no front pockets, no phone. Shit. "Um, I need to check the kitchen. It probably fell out. God, I hope there isn't a body laying on it!" Turning and heading for the kitchen, it's only when I hear his gasp that I realize he followed me in. Well, I guess he'll get right with it or he won't. I have a phone to find. I don't see it in the space where I was fighting, not on the counters. Fuck. One of these assholes is probably laying on it. I have to get a better case for it, if it survives this. Grabbing a body and rolling it over, I groan a little when I don't see the phone. As I reach for the next one, Blair's arm gets there first and hauls the body up in the air, giving it a little shake before dropping it off to the side. He moves to stand next to me, continuing lifting bodies, shaking them, and dropping them off to the side. After the third body, I ask him, "Why are you shaking them?"

He looks down at me, "Two reasons. One, in case the phone is sticking to them." He reaches down and picks up another body to shake, "Two, I kind of hope that one of them is still alive. My dinner plans got cancelled and I'm kind of hungry."

The laughter escapes before I can even think of stopping it. The idea of him finding one alive and gobbling him up seems hilarious for some reason. Even as I am laughing hysterically, the tears flow and I find myself wrapped in Blair's arms. He holds me till the sobs fade away. As he releases me, I realize that I have cried all over his shirt and smeared the blood from my face on him, "Blair, I'm so sorry! I'll get you another shirt. I've ruined this one."

He shakes his head no, "You'll do no such thing. I would happily sacrifice a shirt any time for you. Let's find your phone so you can get to Roman's and get some rest."

I nod and we both stand. He grabs another body and I spot my phone, "Ahah!" I snatch it up and wipe the blood off on my pants. Hitting the button on the side, I am relieved when it lights up and unlocks. Pulling up the contact list and opening a new contact, I type in his first name and hand the phone to him. He drops the body he had just picked up. The head hits the corner of the counter with a crunch that makes me flinch. Taking the phone from me, he enters his number and then his phone rings in his pocket.

He grins at me, "Now I can call to make sure you are safe and happy. You can call me for anything. If you want someone to talk to, need to ruin a shirt, whatever. I am here for you."

I chuckle at the shirt reference, "Thank you, Blair. Maybe we can try the date again, but in the magic sector, so that we don't need to worry about my kitchen becoming a bloodbath before I can cook for you."

"Let me know when you can. I don't care if it is last minute. I'll take you out and show you all the magic sector offers. Maybe you should think about moving in there. For safety."

A raised brow is my only comment on the for safety bit

as I say, "I will think about it. The only problem is that humans bring some of my dogs to me, and a fair number are re-homed with humans."

"You could create a rescue and collect them from the shelter. People can call you and you can collect the dogs or take them to meet them."

"You seem to have thought of everything. I will give it some thought. I am awfully mad at the ghosts for not mentioning that these assholes were throwing poisoned meat over the fence for the dogs."

He nods and puts an arm around me, "Walk me out, please."

"Sir, I would walk damn near anywhere so long as you kept that arm around me."

He makes a pleased sounding rumble deep in his chest. Walking out onto my front porch, he says, "I was hoping I could steal a kiss before I go?"

My arms slip up and around his neck as I lift on my toes to touch my lips to his. His arms wrap around me and lift me as he deepens the kiss. Fire rages through my body as my mouth opens to his, our tongues exploring each other. One of his hands slides down my back to cup my ass and press my body even closer to his. My legs lift and wrap around his body. He groans as my core presses on his hard length through our clothes. I hear Nims bark and we break the kiss. Turning my head in a daze toward the sound, I see her standing in the doorway, barking at Duncan. The haze of lust clears away fairly quickly as what is happening seeps in. Blair chuckles, "Duncan, you have good timing just this once. I probably would have forgotten where we are in another moment or two."

Duncan snarls at him and Nims snarls at Duncan. Blair just laughs as he reaches between us to adjust himself. His knuckles press against my clit and my eyes roll back for a moment as my breath catches. I bring my legs down and he lowers me so my feet are on the porch again. "Blair, the very minute I have time, we are finishing this."

He grins, "I am at your disposal."

Seventeen

Duncan

Over two hours later, we have finally made it to Roman's house. Getting the blood cleaned off the dogs was easier than I expected. They were surprisingly well behaved about the bathing, and by the time we got there, the dogs had dried blood all over. Olivia told them to assume the position, and they lined up. She let us take part, but I could tell it was a slower process for our help. None of it matters. All I can think about is how close she was to dying. She is willful, has no clue about our world, and is so broken. Yet, my every waking minute is nothing but thoughts of her. Seeing her in the shifter's arms caused a rage I didn't know was possible.

The dogs trail behind her, Nims bringing up the rear, as she follows Niall to the rooms assigned to her and the dogs. Roman gave them a suite with a connected room. The first thing she did was march directly to the connected room and throw a blanket over the bed, after she tossed all the pillows into a corner. I watched from the connecting doorway as the dogs jumped onto the bed and curled up next to each other. The ones that couldn't jump were gently lifted onto the bed. Of course, she wouldn't leave them stuck on the bed. She pushed a chair up next to the bed and set pillows where she thought the dogs would jump off the chair.

One pup was found to be hiding under the bed after she counted dogs. She spent twenty minutes with her head under the bed, coaxing the dog out. When it comes out, she cuddles it and tells it that it's okay to be scared while gushing over how brave it was to come out of that safe space.

This is why. This is why the very thought that she might die sent terror racing through my body. I don't think I have ever felt fear so great as when I was fighting to get to her tonight. If she hadn't drunk from one of them, she would have died there. I saw the man that ran after he realized what she was doing. That will not help anything. I'll have to make sure Roman knows.

The only thing I know for sure is a world without her isn't one I want to be in. That scares me almost as much as the thought of her dying. I am watching her still when she nearly walks into me, stopping short. My hands have caught her arms to stop her fall before I even registered the desire to catch her. Oh Duncan, lad, you are well and truly fucked.

Olivia stares up at me, saying, "What are you doing still here? Don't you have somewhere to be? A place to brood?"

She shrugs off my hands and shoves past me. "You should be in your own room, not mine."

I am right behind her when she spins around and her breath catches as I say, "This is exactly where I need to be. You could have died tonight, and I can't take the chance that someone could try that again." My hands go to her arms, stroking them. "I need you to be safe."

The scent of her arousal permeates the room as she whispers, "Why?"

"Because I need you, Olivia." Her lips are parted, and I close most of the space between us. "May I kiss you Olivia?"

She swallows and says, "Yes." That answer was all I needed. My arms go round her as my lips claim hers, the kiss reassuring everything in me that she really is still here, still alive.

Her hands are exploring my back as I break the kiss to say, "I want you. If you don't want to be taken right now, you need to tell me. I'll go sleep on the couch, just say the word."

She draws in a deep breath, inhaling slowly through her nose before she says, "Fuck me, Duncan. I might die if you leave me like this."

Her consent was all I needed. Lifting her up, I head for the bed. Nims stands, gives me a dirty look and heads for the couch.

Setting her on her feet next to the bed, I work at taking her clothes off without ripping them off like I want to do. Every inch of creamy skin revealed a glorious. Curves everywhere and she smells of sandalwood and books. Kneeling before her, I worship her the only way I know how, with lips and tongue. Lifting one of her legs and hooking it over my shoulder, I run my tongue from her entrance to her clit as I grip her hips. Her body shivers and I press my lips to her clit, kissing it gently. Her hands thread their way into my hair as I suck lightly on her. The leg she is standing on shakes, and I press her back onto the bed. Her hands never leave my hair and it keeps me right where I want to be as she lays back across the bed. My cock is a little pained at still being confined to my pants. Keeping up the ministrations on her clit, I reach down and free myself. Now that one hand is off her hips, I know just what to do with it. Her little moans stop on a gasp as I press two fingers into her. My tongue goes into overdrive on that little clit of hers as her hips buck and grind on my fingers. Curling them just a bit so they hit the right spot sends her right over the edge and her slick entrance clamps down on my fingers in waves. Easing back from her clit as her fingers release my hair, I withdraw my fingers and stand. She watches through hooded eyes as I lick her off my fingers. "Goddamn, you taste so fucking good."

Shoving my pants down with one hand and snatching my shirt off with the other has me ready to join her in orgasmic bliss, when she comes for me again. Taking my cock in my hand, I step forward and rub it along her slit. Every time I touch her clit, she moans and presses on the head of my cock. Lining up with her entrance and pressing in just far enough to stay, I reach and grab her legs to put up against my chest. She moans as I push the rest of the way in. Bending my arms at the elbows, I shrug her legs off so they fall to rest on my arms while I have her thighs gripped in my hands. "Touch yourself."

Her eyes fly open and she says, "What?"

"Touch yourself. I'm not moving till I see you rubbing that little clit of yours." She narrows her eyes at me and starts to rock her hips. I counter by withdrawing from her till the head is just touching her fiery core.

She groans. "I can't do that. I can't let someone see me doing that."

I want to hunt down whoever put this shame in her and tear them into tiny little pieces. Instead, a change of tack is called for here. "Please, let me see you touch yourself. I don't know what asshole told you that no one should see you touch yourself, but I promise you that a real person finds it hot. Man, woman, they. We all pretty unilaterally find it hot unless we are not interested in sex. Now," I say as I move my hips forward ever so slightly, "please touch yourself for me. I desperately want to see your face as you make yourself come on my cock."

A little smile plays on her face as she slides one hand down the middle of her body, through the curls on her mound, to stop with two fingers on her clit. I am hypnotized by the movement, even as my hips move to bury my cock in her hot, velvety core. Looking up at her face, her mouth is open just a little and her eyes have closed. Her fingers are moving faster and I match my pace to them. Watching her expression is so hot I have to strain to keep from sailing right over the edge. Her mouth forms a little oh as her fingers go mad on that clit. I do my part, fucking her hard and fast. Seeing the moment when her orgasm starts on her face and that's more than I can take. I fly off the cliff into a million pieces as I watch her still coming. My hips slow as she comes down from outer space, eventually stopping buried as deep as I can go.

Her eyes open and search my face. "Olivia, that was the sexiest thing I have ever gotten to take part in. I would love it if you would touch yourself anywhere you please if you agree to having sex with me again."

She smiles and I grin down at her. "Stay put. I'll get something to clean you up."

Eighteen

Olivia

I know he is gone even before I open my eyes. Nims is in her usual spot. No one else is in this bed besides me. Opening my eyes, I look around to verify anyway. I don't understand. Why would he do this when he could easily have had sex with anyone else? Why catch me in a weak moment, when the rest of the time he works hard at making me angry with him?

Maybe he is just one of those jerks that wants what he doesn't have? That must be it. Well, it's fine. I'll tell Blair what happened, because I won't hide this from him. Besides, I think his kiss and the fire he started might have had something to do with it. Yes. That's exactly it. And that means this is definitely nothing to cry about. It was just a weak moment on my part, one that Duncan took advantage of. He could probably tell I was still turned on from Blair earlier. This, this was nothing.

Getting out of bed, I go to my bags and pull out some clothing. I am just getting my shirt straight when the door to the suite opens to reveal Duncan pushing a cart with dishes of food for the dogs on it. My jaw drops. Recovering from the shock, I ask, "What are you doing?"

He shrugs, "Helping you feed the horde."

Even as I help to set out dishes for them, I just don't get it. What is he doing back in here? Was he really out there just for this? Did I read the situation wrong? Oh God, what if I read the situation wrong? Now what? What do I do? I still want Blair. But Duncan is in my bed already. This is all so confusing. The last of the dog's dishes are out and I excuse myself to the bathroom before he can start talking to me. I know this won't put it off forever, but it gives me a chance to wash my face and pull myself together. I am going to have to talk to them both. Fucked if I know what is going to happen from there. Sex Ed class did not cover this. I need to read some books on this stuff. I know there are relationships like this in the book world, but are there any in real life? Is it possible? Is it even feasible to have a vampire and a shifter as my lovers at the same time? Does that make me a whore? I know what my parents would think. But, they think I should let that prick Sprenger perform an exorcism on me. Maybe, maybe I need to let go of some of the things they said made for a proper, godly woman?

On that thought, I exit the bathroom and find all the dogs have finished eating and are ready to go for a walk. I look at Duncan. "Where are we walking them?"

"One of the gardens. Roman has assigned someone to scoop everything left behind three times nightly, so you won't have to worry about anything piling up."

He opens the door and I step out, Nims right beside me. He follows and then guides us down to the proper door, two neat lines of dogs trailing behind us. Once they are outside, all bets are off. Even Nims joins in the fun, running and playing in this new place. Which leaves me alone with Duncan. He nudges my arm with his shoulder as we walk. "Penny for your thoughts?"

"My thoughts are a little chaotic right now. I think I need to know some things from you. What are you looking for with me? What was last night?"

He chuckles, "I like to think last night was good for both of us."

So thankful vampires don't blush, I say, "Yes, but aside from that?"

He says, "I am unsure. I went into this annoyed that I was being sent to be a bodyguard for you. I thought it was beneath my station. That idea has since been blasted from my brain. And by beneath my station, I mean I am highly trained for this. I didn't feel like you were in a lot of danger and this was definitely going to be a really boring detail. As it happens, I was wrong. I wasn't expecting to find myself wanting you so much, to find myself so worried about your safety, beyond the job. When you, when you were so close. During the fight, I thought you might." He pauses and takes a deep breath. Looking off in the distance, he continues, "When I thought you might die, it was the worst moment of my entire life. And that has been a lot longer than you have been alive. I haven't felt this way about anyone in a very long time. The only person I cared about this way was my wife. She is long gone, though. I thought I was done. Had one great love, she chose to die, and that was that. I'm not sure what to do here. I know I want you and I have some feelings for you. Could it grow into more? I think so. But now the question becomes, what do you want from this?"

I place a hand on his arm and stop him as I turn to face him. "Why did your wife choose to die?"

He looks down at me. "She was a devout Christian. When I was turned, she was horrified. But she believed that marriage was for so long as you both lived and that to leave me would be the greater sin for her. She loved me too, or maybe I just like to think she did. I begged her to allow them to turn her so we could stay together. She refused every time, saying that she wouldn't give up her immortal soul for anyone."

"I'm so sorry. That must have been hard for you. Were yo with her till she died?"

He nods and starts walking again. "I was. I was there with her when she passed. She told me I had been a good, faithful husband and she was sorry that she wouldn't see me in the afterlife. That it was a shame that I was damned to hell for all eternity. I was mad at her for a long time after that."

"Why would you be mad at her?"

"Because the church showed up to kill me right after her funeral."

I can't help but gasp. Of all the things I thought he would say, this was not on the list. "You're joking, right? You stayed with her and were a good husband till she died and she turned you in to the church?"

He shoves his hands in his pockets as he walks. His face is turned from me and his shoulders are hunched as he says, "Yes. The one I questioned said that they had known about me for years and only let me live because she held me in check while they studied me."

"What did you do?"

"I killed the entire church clergy. They knew about me, had been studying me. For years. I checked all their correspondence and hunted down anyone that might know about me. It occupied a few years of my time."

"That must've really hurt. I'm sorry. I can understand why you would withdraw from relationships after that. We should take the dogs inside. They are probably ready for morning naps."

He nods and we head for the door as I whistle for the dogs.

* * *

Duncan

I have to come clean. I can't let her decide about whether she wants to go any further with this not knowing. The dogs are gathering around us as we walk slowly toward the door. Deep breath, "You need to know some things. I didn't want to find anyone, but even before I was sent to guard you, I could not ignore you. The vampire world is not a safe place. Especially if you have any sort of standing. This is why Roman is still single. Having a special someone makes you vulnerable. It is one of the downsides to being a vampire. This is something you would have learned if you had become a vampire in the conventional way." Taking her hand, I tug her lightly to a stop.

She is looking down and away from me. I touch her chin and she lifts her face to look at me. Nims has sat close to us and is watching me as I say, "I am not impartial with you. As I said, even before the witches made their demands, I couldn't take my eyes off you when you came into the bar. I told myself that seeing you was enough, that I could make that enough. No one would ever guess how much I wanted you. You would be safe because I was strong enough to stay away from you. I can't pretend that is true anymore. Watching you from across the room isn't enough anymore. Even though it adds to the danger you are in. I need to be near you. If you say the word, I will back off. I can ask," I grit my teeth because I don't fucking want to say this part, "Roman to assign someone else. Possibly even Niall. I want to stay with you more than anything, but only if you want that, too." Tears roll down her cheeks and all I can think is, fuck, I broke her.

<h1 style="text-align:center">Nineteen</h1>

Olivia

Listening to him breaks my heart. He might actually care for me, and I'm not good enough to keep anyone. They always end up leaving me and I just can't take that again. I've only known him a short time, and it hurts already. I can't. Looking at him, I tell him, "I'm sorry, I just can't do this."

He nods, "I understand, it's Blair. Or Niall."

Shaking my head no, I tell him, "I just can't do this. I don't know how to do any of this."

Snatching my hand from his, I turn and head for the door. Nims at my side and the rest of them on my heels as I walk away from someone who wants too much too fast. I thought maybe I could dip my toes in the water, but this is terrifying. I can't fall for someone! My life is good. I don't want to feel like I did those first few years. I have to get out of here. And I'll just send a letter to the witches. I'll leave and everything will be fine. The witches won't start a war because I left on my own. I am stuffing my suitcase when Niall walks in and stops. "What are you doing?"

"I'm leaving. I can't stay here. Can't do this. It just isn't going to work for me."

Niall comes closer. "Honey, why are you crying? What happened out there?"

"It's nothing. Everything. I can't let him get close to me and find out that I'm not good enough for anyone. Going through that again, it would kill me."

He scowls at me as I zip the case. "I thought you were braver than that. Hurt is a part of life, pain reminds us how to be human. I think you are making a mistake."

Nodding, I tell him, "You might be right. But it's my mistake to make. I am going to take my chances on my own. And I'll make sure the witches know I left on my own and that none of you are to blame. I don't want there to be any repercussions for you and your family."

He hugs me, and I hug him back as he says, "This could be your family too, if you would let it happen."

My heart breaks in my chest and I step back, out of his embrace as I put my hand over my heart like it will stop the pain. "That's what I'm afraid of. Family always leaves." Grabbing my suitcase from the bed, I step around Niall and head for the front door, Nims and the dogs trailing behind me. The dogs and I are out in the car before anyone even thinks to stop us. I breathe a sigh of relief as I drive out of the gates. I need to stop by the house and pick up a couple of things, then we are heading somewhere. Before I get out of the car, I send a quick message to Blair, telling him what is happening. I'll figure out where after we are out of Inverness. The house is silent and dark, it reminds me of the tombs they show on tv. I let the dogs out into the backyard as a text comes in from Blair. He wants me to stay put and wait for him. I text him back that he isn't changing my mind. Shoving my phone back in my pocket as I turn from the back door and head for my bedroom, I leave it open so the dogs can wander in when they finish.

I am halfway to the closet when my bedroom door closes. I spin around to find four preachers standing in my bedroom. Dammit! This is what happens when you don't pay attention to your surroundings, Olivia! Three of them come at me while the fourth stays by the door. Fuck. The first one swings at my face. I lean back to avoid getting hit and the other two grab my arms. They are a lot stronger than they should be, but I manage to kick one in the knee and send it bending the wrong way. He lets go as he falls to the floor, howling. Something big hits the bedroom door and the guy in front of it puts his back against the door as he shouts for the others to hurry. I hit the one still holding my arm in the face and the guy barely moves. What the hell kind of humans are these, anyway? The guy that tried to hit me the first time lands a punch in my gut. Jokes on you fucker, I saw it coming. Swinging at him, I hear another loud thump against the door as my fist doesn't quite hit where I was aiming, getting his shoulder as he dips to one side. I have got to learn to fight and how to dodge these damned crosses. One hits my thigh, going to the bone, excruciating pain floods my body.

Duncan

"I know you said I need to guard her, but I'm telling you, it can't be me."

Roman sighs. "I don't care what your reason is. You are her bodyguard until she doesn't need one."

"I know it doesn't matter to you. It matters to her. She needs her bodyguard to not be me."

Roman is accustomed to his orders being followed without argument and he turns now to look directly at me, his brows drawn down and his mouth set. He stands and says, "Duncan, I am going to pretend you aren't arguing with me because you are my favorite and best enforcer. This is the one time you are getting an explanation. Listen close. You are her bodyguard. Period. I will not assign anyone else. I know you think that no one can tell you have had an attraction to her since well before this situation started, but I know." My entire being is paralyzed from the bomb he just dropped as he continues, "I am fully aware of how dangerous it is to care for someone in our world. We marry for connections here because of it. Your desire to keep her safe is why you are the best man for the job. I know it will hurt you and that you are strong enough to withstand the pain. She is going to be one of us. You will both need to figure something out. She needs you and you are going to be there, no matter what she wants. Do you understand now?"

Before I can answer, Niall runs in, "She is leaving. You have to go after her!"

Roman glares at the both of us. "Niall, why didn't you stop her? Duncan, fetch her back here. Now."

Never taking my gaze off Niall, I tell Roman, "It should be Niall."

Niall rolls his eyes, "My gods, you are dumb! She is afraid you will abandon her, just like everyone else. And here you are, doing just that! You know her history!"

Roman adds, "You get your ass out there and you bring her back. I don't care how it happens, but you make it happen. If she dies and we are to be wiped out by the witches, I am flaying the skin off your body first."

His face is set, there is no changing his mind now. With a turn, I leave the office, heading for Olivia's. I can't say I don't want to. I want to be where she is more than anything. Standing in that office trying to do what she wanted was tearing my heart into small pieces. Skipping the car, I run toward her house. She can't be that far ahead.

Stepping onto her porch, something doesn't feel right. I hear all the dogs barking out back. The new back door is closed. I turn toward the stairs and I hear a loud thump. There are parts of a man on the stairs. Fuck, they must have been here waiting to ambush her. I hear another thump and I hurry up the stairs to find Nims in the hall looking at the door to her bedroom with rage. She doesn't like me and I don't know if she is in control. Deciding to err with caution, since I can hear right now is the cacophony of dogs, I speak to her before I approach her."Nims, are you ok?"

She turns her head, narrows her eyes at me and snorts. Then pointedly looks at the door and back at me, growling low in her throat. I've never in my life felt so dumb as when I am around this dog. Drawing close to her, I tell her, "On two. We hit the door on two." I swear her facial expression says get on with it stupid. "One, two!" As we hit the door, the sound of glass shattering and a wolf growling reaches us.

We land on top of the door and the man that was in front of it. Nims and the giant wolf have both leapt over and are fighting with the men attacking Olivia. I get off the door, and reaching under it, I grab the man. He is crying and appears to have soiled himself. Breaking his neck takes nothing, and I toss him to the side as I turn to face Olivia. She is still grappling with the one man the beasts didn't decide looked like nice chew toys. A few steps have me behind him and I grab the back of his very starched and proper preacher collar. He makes pleasant gagging noises as I pull him up until I break his neck. The cleaners are going to have plenty to do when they get here. I don't want to add to the mess.

Twenty

Olivia

Shit. Blair and Duncan are here. And they helped me fight of the ambush that was waiting for me up here. It's just that much more reason why I should leave. Duncan crosses his arms over his chest, watching me as I wait for Blair to finish shifting. The giant black wolf that lives inside him is beautiful. The blue eyes that looked accusingly at me from that wolf's face were all Blair and I just know he has opinions on my idea of leaving here. Glancing over at Duncan, I think he is just waiting to get rid of Blair before he yells at me about not leaving.

And yet, somehow, all I can think about is how standing in a room with blood everywhere seems to fade into the background with them in it. Blair, the very definition of tall, dark, and stunning. His blue eyes are like ice against his ebony skin and a thick, muscular build that didn't make me feel like I would break him by accident. Duncan, swarthy and stout, his muscles less on display because he is bulky in general. Neither one smiling, their frowns and anger mirroring each other more than I think Duncan would appreciate.

It's all I can do not to focus on the throbbing between my legs as the two of them advance on me, stopping only a foot or so away. Blair growls down at me and suddenly Nims is pressed against the front of my legs. Blair is startled as he looks down at her. "Oh, Nims, you don't have to worry. I wouldn't hurt her for anything. I only plan to yell at her." He pauses as she pointedly looks at Duncan.

Duncan eyes her, saying, "I am still not a threat, Nims. The only threats here are Olivia's ideas about leaving."

Nims looks less than reassured but sits. On my feet. Blair chuckles and reaches down to pat her head. Straightening, he looks at me and butterflies start a rave in my vagina at the fierce look in his eye. "Olivia, what in the hell do you think you are doing? Why didn't you call me before you left the vampire monstrosity? What if I had been too late?"

"Then the problem would be solved by now. Well, it probably would have started a war for the vampires, but I get the feeling they wouldn't mind a minor war to alleviate their monotony."

Blair sighs, "Listen, you can't leave here. The witches think you are needed for something. Come stay with me. You won't have—"

Duncan interrupts, moving his hand in a slicing motion. He says, "Absolutely not! She is coming back to Roman's place."

Blair turns to face Duncan and stands at his full height. "She decides what she does, as long as her choice is to come to safety with one of us. You don't get to choose for her."

Duncan narrows his eyes as he plants his feet. "She goes with me."

This is going nowhere good. Slipping between them, I try not to be overwhelmed by their combined scents as I push them back from each other. "Stop it now. We are not doing this. Blair, I'll come to your house. Duncan, tell Roman that I will talk to the witches and make this all right."

Duncan groans. "This isn't about the witches! We will lose face as a region if someone else guards you."

Shit. That complicates things. I don't want to cause them problems. But I need to be away from Duncan right now, though. I can't be alone with him, knowing what he wants from me. What if I fucked up and said yes?

"I see. I will stay at Blair's home for two days. Then I will come back. I, I need some time away from you."

I can feel Blair relax under my hand as I say that. A sad look flashes across Duncan's face but is quickly gone. My heart breaks a little more for hurting him. He says, "Very well. I will be nearby and I will let Roman know. So he doesn't decide to hunt you down."

Blair tenses and I feel the growl in his chest more than hear it. Pressing my fingers into his chest seems to keep him eased back as I tell Duncan, "Good. Thank you. I appreciate that."

He nods, turning away and stops. "I'll be downstairs. Waiting to go with you to Blair's home."

Rolling my eyes, I decide that answering him will be pointless. Turning to face Blair, it is an effort to drag my eyes up to his. The t-shirt he has on does very little to hide the muscles under it. "So, um, I will come to your place."

He grins, his hands going to my waist and pulling me close to him. "You'll sleep in my room. If you like, I'll sleep there with you. If you are a good girl, maybe we can finish what we started."

"About that. We should talk before that."

He laughs, "Why? Do you think it will offend me that you had sex with Duncan?"

"How did you know?"

"Even if the sexual tension between the two of you wasn't nearly visible, I would still smell the mingling of your scents."

"But I showered!"

"Scents still mingle for a time after that. You would need to wash with something more pungent to keep a wolf from knowing what you've been doing. I don't mind though. We have made no promises. I want you for my own, but I will always respect your decisions." His hands are like fire on my back and being pressed against the length of him is doing terrible things to my ability to think about anything other than getting railed by him. He grins down at me. "Besides, I can smell how much more turned on you are since he left the room. Hella balm to the ego of a man that hasn't yet tasted you."

Oh my. That rumbly voice of his is going to be the end of these panties. Pushing myself away from him is almost as hard as he is. Oh lord, I need to not think about this. "I, uh, we need to get going."

He leans in, whispering, "I'll text you my address. Get your things together and I will feast when you arrive."

All I can do is stand there still as is possible while shivers of electricity run through my body. When my eyes open again, he is gone. Nims is still sitting, watching everything. Shaking off the trance, I tell her, "You should be glad you don't have to deal with this. My concentration is shit and I still have to deal with Duncan."

She grins at me, and I can't help but laugh.

I am standing in a room painted with the blood of murderous preachers, surrounded by their lifeless corpses. Yet, all I seem to be concerned with is getting railed. My phone pings. A quick check shows his address. Moving into the closet, I open the secret compartment and pull out the little metal box. Closing up the space, I head downstairs to face Duncan.

* * *

To put him off a little longer, I go directly to the back door and open it, allowing all my very concerned dogs into the house. Nims chuffs lightly at them and they calm down. I don't know what I would do without her. Her love is what has kept me going all this time. I could lose it all, so long as I have her by my side, I can make it through anything.

Duncan is silent as we walk past him and out the front door to get the dogs loaded. When I finish, he is standing in the door to the passenger side. He seats himself in the vehicle as I look at the house one more time. I really love this place. Maybe I can come back here one day. It's only when I pull away from the curb that Duncan starts talking. "What do you think you are doing? You know Roman is pissed about this, don't you?"

"I'm sure he is. But this is my life, and he has as much

control over it as he ever will. Even if he adopts me into the family, he still doesn't get to control me."

"He can just send people to collect you if he chooses."

"He could. But is that the really wise thing to do? He could try remembering that I am a person, the same as he is. He doesn't get to take over my life."

"You should be with the vampires. We can keep you safe if you will just stay with us. And," he twists in the seat to look at my face. "Is it really so terrible that I want more with you? I wouldn't force you. I can accept no. Why do you need to run away?"

I was hoping he would just leave it alone. My hands grip the wheel a little tighter. What do I tell him? The truth? That I can't handle someone becoming important to me and then leaving me for some stupid reason? Or lie and tell him I just don't feel that way about him? "I just don't feel that way about you, that's all."

He snorts, "You should not attempt to lie to save your life. You are incredibly bad at it. Small children will cry if you tell them Santa is real."

My jaw drops. I can't believe he said that! "Small children do not cry when I tell them Santa is real! And I wasn't lying. I don't feel that way about you. About us."

He sits back in his seat and remains silent as I navigate the rest of the way to Blair's home. Once the car is in park, I get out and move to the passenger side to let the dogs out into the yard. Duncan is standing next to the door waiting for me. My feet slow and stop before I get too close. I can smell his cologne and that scent particular to him. It makes me want to lean into him, but I hold myself back with an iron will. "Plan to move so I can let the dogs out?"

He smirks. "I know you care. I think you are just scared. So am I. Caring for anyone in this world is scary. The vampire world is vicious and predatory. I stayed away from you for so long. But I'm done playing it safe. I will keep you safe. I know you care. And I know you want me." He reaches out and pulls me against him, lifting me off my feet. My hand goes to his chest, so I can push him away. Instead, I remember how those pecs felt under my hands and then he is kissing me. His tongue taking possession of my mouth. My body responds before I can formulate a thought.

Nims barks, and I come to my senses, pushing him back. "Stop! We aren't doing this! Go away Duncan. I am here, I am safe. We will not be a thing. I told you no."

He grins down at me. "You don't mean it. And I am going to be here when you get tired of pretending you don't want me."

"Today is not that day, vampire. She said to put her down."

This is not happening. Looking to the right confirms that Blair is, in fact, standing next to us. Super.

Duncan releases me, lowering me to stand on my own. "No. Yesterday was the day. Maybe tomorrow will be the day, too." Somehow, the ground has not opened to swallow me whole. One day I am going to get to quit being grateful that vampires can't blush. Today is not that day either.

Blair snarls at him, "You need to put some respect in your mouth when you speak about her. Unless you want me to put it there for you?"

Oh shit. Jumping between them, I put a hand on each of these big chests and try to stay focused. "Duncan, go home. I am here to stay. Two days. Remember? You go, find something to do."

He eyes me, one brow raised. "Worried that we'll fight? Don't. I can take him."

The audacity in this man. I push back on Blair as he growls and starts forward. "No Duncan. I'm worried that I am going to have to tell on you to Roman. I have his number now. So go. If you can't respect my wish for you to go, at least respect that Roman is going to tear you a new asshole for starting shit with the shifters."

He glares at me. "Fine. I'll be across the street."

I nearly fall when he spins on his heel and runs across the street, but Blair catches my hand. "Thank you. Let's get my dogs out of the car." He nods and I open the door, letting them all spill out to explore this yard. Nims snorts at me as she exits. "I will get something sorted so that you can open the door. Promise." Hitting the button to lock my car, I slam the door and turn away from the car. Blair is there waiting, a half smile on his face as he watches me.

"Looks like you two had a pleasant talk."

"I don't know that it was really a pleasant talk. I told him that I am not interested in more with him and he isn't willing to accept that."

Blair shrugs, "I can see why he would have problems accepting it. Especially with the way you kiss. That was hot."

Blink. I can't do more than blink for a moment as my brain processes what he just said. It was hot? "I'm sorry. I think I misheard you. You didn't say that it was hot the way I kissed him back, right?"

He chuckles and slips an arm around me, guiding me

toward his front door. "I did say that. But let's talk inside. I'm sure the dogs will be ready to eat soon." The dogs fall in with us as we walk toward his house. It's a simple house. Blue door with matching shutters and dark brick walls. It has a small porch, more like a large entry. He opens the door and we wait as all the dogs enter. I walk in after them and Blair follows, closing the door behind himself. He leads the way into the kitchen, and as I round the corner, I stop to stare. The kitchen is enormous. Lots of open space, light, and a large island in the middle with sixteen dog dishes lined up. "Blair, you got dishes for my dogs?"

He smiles as he pulls out food for them. "I did. I just stopped by the shop and pilfered a few. No big deal. And I know what you feed them, so it wasn't difficult to bring some of that back with me."

"How are you so perfect?"

His smile grows as he says, "I'm a shifter. We're all perfect." He chuckles as he fills dishes. "I think it is a social difference. The shifter community is about the whole, not the individual. We want all of us to succeed and to be happy. This is probably helped by the fact that women are rarely born or changed into shifters. Because of this, our people have moved away from the monogamous standard. Women in our world choose to have as many or as few partners as they can handle."

"Oh. I thought that was just a romance novel thing."

"No. It happens in a lot more places than certain factions like to imagine. I believe some of the humans are following a similar model now."

"So you are fine with it if you are not the only person I am with?"

"Yes. So long as that is your choice. If you tell Duncan to go away and he won't, I will make him if you want me to do so. I didn't mean to let him goad me out there. It was poorly done of me. I wouldn't have minded ripping his arm off and beating him with it for a while." I can't help but laugh at that picture as he sets the filled dishes out for the dogs. Nims dish is saved for last and he puts her near my feet. Coming to lean against the island on the side of me further from Nims, he says, "That said, I would like to ask what the parameters are for my behavior. I know I said I would feast on you when you arrived, but if you don't want that, it isn't required."

His words cause a shiver in my body. "I think I would like to be a feast."

"Mhmm. Will we be moving toward a relationship or do you want to pretend we will be nothing more than friends who have sex?"

"Huh, that's an interesting way to put that. I said yes to you that day because I don't think you are going to run off and ditch me for specious reasons. I feel safe with you in ways that I don't with most people. You feel like you won't abandon me just because I am not who you want me to be. Or because I don't fit into the world you live in. I know the shifter world is a lot different from anything I have experienced. My human life was heavily based on appearances. We needed to be the best Christians when people could see us. Always fully supporting the church and taking part. It didn't matter that I hated it. It didn't matter that I moved out and avoided my parents rather than going to church with them. What mattered was that the church people might find out they had accepted me during a time when I was struggling and they couldn't have that. No, that would be embarrassing for the family." Blair's arms wrap around me and I realize I left on a tangent and didn't even answer his question. "Shit. I'm sorry. The answer is yes, more. And also, I don't know if I can be trusted with Duncan. He is infuriating, and apparently I like that because I am damaged."

He chuckles. "I can live with that. Shifter men are accustomed to not being the only man in a relationship. Now the question becomes, will Duncan be able to live with that or will he try to take you from me?"

"I don't know. But today, I don't want to worry about that. Let's give my dogs some treats and some time outside before the sun comes up. Then you can show me where I get to sleep."

His hands caress my arms as he releases me. I can feel him watching me as I grab treats from the bag I definitely did not carry in, but is here anyway. "Thank you for bringing in my bag. I thought I was going to have to get it from the car."

Blair chuckles, saying, "That wasn't me. Duncan did it while we have been talking. I let him think he was unnoticed because he wasn't hurting anything and he probably wanted to see you."

"Oh. How much did he hear?"

"Enough to know he has some choices to make."

"I suppose that is good. Now I don't have to break it to him gently. Shall we take the dogs out front or to the back?"

"Front. Let Duncan see you one more time before he has to sit on his hands, knowing I've got you in mine."

Oh my, that set off an entire flock of butterflies in my

vagina. It might make me a slut in the human world, because I was with Duncan yesterday, but I can't wait to have Blair. The one thing he and Duncan have in common, besides me, is that neither one looks like I will break him in half. I know they can both pick me up with ease and I don't have to worry about suffocating them if I sit on one of their faces. Blair lifts his head and sniffs the air, looking at me with a grin. "I can't wait either. Hurry up with those treats."

Suddenly it is a sprint to get the dogs their treats and get them back inside. They cooperate with Nims help. I swear she is the best of dogs ever. There won't be another like her. I am so glad she was turned the night I was, because I would be lost without her.

Back inside, he leads the way to a bedroom that he set up for my dogs. It has a bed and various cushions strewn about. It also has a few dishes of water in case they get thirsty. Nims gives me a nudge with her shoulder and presses her face into my hand. Kneeling beside her, I give her scratches and cuddles as she presses herself against me. Once her cuddle quota is filled, she gives me a swipe up my cheek with her tongue and moves off to claim her space on the bed. After all the dogs are comfy in their spots, we retreat from the room, leaving the door open.

Blair slips an arm around me. "Let's get you to my bed." He leads me to the next door and pushes it open to reveal his bedroom. It's neat, everything in order and a bed dominating the room. No headboard or footboard, just this immense bed in the middle of the room. Pillows lined up across one end and what looks like a silky comforter.

"Silk comforter? I like it."

He scoops me up into his arms and carries me toward the bed. "Now is the time to say something if you want to go directly to sleep. I've been waiting to get you here since the first time you walked into the store."

"You sure know how to flatter a woman. I would prefer to get railed thoroughly before I sleep. Chase away the years I went without."

He lays me on the bed, so gently. I'm a little concerned that railed might have been too strong a word. "What's your safe word?"

"Safe word?"

"If you really want me to stop, you say the safe word. Sometimes the brain gets stuck on repeat." He is over me now, one arm braced as the other unbuttons my shirt. "No, don't stop becomes no, no, no, and I can't tell if you mean it. Now, what is your safe word?"

"I've never had sex good enough to make my brain get stuck. That happens?"

"Focus, Olivia." He pushes the two sides of my shirt out of the way. "What. Is. Your. Safe. Word." His head dips to the valley between my breasts. He inhales deeply and then licks from there up my neck, stopping just below my ear. He nibbles my ear and sends little frissons of pleasure through my body. "I need that word, Olivia."

"Um, oh god, uh. Watermelon. Watermelon is the safe word."

He nips at my neck and pleasure spreads from the bite. "Why watermelon?"

"Because I don't really like watermelon. Never been a fan."

He lifts my arms above my head. "Keep your hands up

there until I say otherwise, or you say watermelon." I nod and he dips down, pressing his lips to mine, his tongue seeking entrance that I grant immediately. He swirls his tongue around mine and I put my hands together, clenching them to keep from bringing them down to stroke all of him. His hand comes to my throat and glides down my chest, pushing the cups of my bra under my breasts as he kisses and nips his way down my body. His lips close over a nipple and my body arches up with the electric charges running through it. He bites my nipple lightly, and a moan escapes my lips. I'm panting and I don't even need to breathe.

His hand goes to the waistband of my pants as he takes the other nipple in his mouth, sucking hard on it. My shoulders are barely touching the bed as my body tries to push that breast further into his mouth. Then a hand cups my sex and I think I could come now. But he just uses it to gently press me back down on the bed. He releases my nipple and I whimper in protest until he bites his way down my body, pushing my legs open to settle himself between them. He snakes his arms around my thighs and grips them tightly. Dimly, I wonder why until his tongue licks from my vagina to my clit and my body twitches. His tongue and lips focus on my clit and I can't help but thrash on the bed as the pleasure overwhelms all reason.

He takes his lips from my clit and blows gently on it, "You taste so fucking fantastic. I could lap at you all day. You are such a good girl, taking all these sensations. Now come for me."

I start to say something and his mouth clamps on my clit, sucking hard as his tongue flicks over again and again. My entire body is shaking, moans and shouts ripping from my throat. The wave of pleasure crashes down on me, breaking me into thousands of shining points. Just when I think I am coming down, his lips releasing my super sensitive clit, he presses his tongue against it and starts wiggling it back and forth. "Oh god, oh no, there's nothing left, oh fuck! Oh, no, fuck me, I can't! Noooo!" The next orgasm hits me so hard and fast, my body raises up from the bed and he follows, never letting up on the pressure. When I come back to earth, he is kissing my thighs and making a noise that sounds suspiciously like purring. "I understand why you insisted on a safe word."

The purring stops and he says, "Ready for more?"

"I am not ready for more of your mouth on my pussy. Unless, are you only able to do that? Are other things not possible?"

"Are you trying to ask me if my dick is functional?"

"I wouldn't put it quite like that, but close enough."

He growls at me as he backs away, off the bed to snatch his shirt over his head. Watching him get undressed is a lot hotter than I ever imagined watching a man take his clothing off could be. His hands go to the fastening of his pants and I am mesmerized. Opening his pants and pushing them down till they drop to the floor reveals a thick, long cock that I can't wait to have in me. It's so hard it is pulsing with his heartbeat. I wonder if he would be offended if I drank a little from him while... Maybe that's a second time we have sex kind of conversation? He steps out of his pants and crawls up the bed, stopping just as he gets between my knees. His hands are like fire when he sets them on my knees and slides them down toward the juncture of my thighs.

"Are you ready? Remember your safe word?"

"I am and I do."

"Say it for me."

"All right, but if you stop right now, I'll be mad. The safe word is watermelon."

"Good girl." He leans down as his hands stroke up my body. He slows to nibble various spots before he pauses to lavish attention on my breasts. My hands are still where he left them. I haven't thought of them till now. I bring my hands down to explore the smoothness of his bald head and down to his shoulders, where they stop as the head of his cock finds my slick entrance. My hips move of their own accord, trying to get more of him inside me. When I groan in frustration, he pushes in, sinking himself deep into me as I gasp, my fingers becoming a little claw like as I hang on to him. He holds himself completely still, buried in me. Opening my eyes, I look up at him. "Why aren't you moving?"

He growls at me. "You feel real damn good. I don't want to embarrass myself with a minute man performance."

Something wicked in me rears up and I say, "Oh? So it wouldn't help if I did something like this, right?" Without moving away from him, I twist my hips as far as I can one way and then back the other. His eyes roll back in his head as he moans.

"Fucking hell, Olivia. How do you feel this good?"

With feedback like that, the wicked part of me switches the movement of my hips so they rocking back and forth. A snarl rips out of Blair's throat as his arms go round me and snatch me up so I am on his lap. He adjusts his hands, so he is supporting my body with two hands full of my ass and he lifts me up a little higher. He rails the hell right out of me, and all I can do is hang on. I feel another orgasm building and then he bites my shoulder. Every point where his teeth are in contact with my body sends electricity shooting through my body. The orgasm hits me with a ferocity I didn't know possible, as this man holds my body up while he fucks me hard and fast. He slams into me one more time and releases my shoulder as he shouts with the force of his orgasm.

He gently lays us down on our sides as our breathing returns to normal. "I don't care if you need to have other men, too. I just want to be one of them."

"Duly noted. I need to clean up before sunrise, though. I am still young enough that the sunrise makes me sleepy."

Twenty-One

Callum

Closing the book, I take a few minutes of silence with my eyes closed. I hate leaving a book world and immediately being confronted by the real world. It ruins the book afterglow. This horror novel was fantastic. It's almost like the author is one of us...

Flipping to the inside back cover, I look at the picture. It is a woman. She looks so familiar. Why do I feel like I met her somewhere? A dim memory surfaces. Walking through a park on my way to the party that went so wrong. A dirty woman covered in blood, curled up with a dog. I gave her my blood, and she refused to leave the damn dog. I was supposed to go find her the next night!

Looking closer at the picture, I notice she looks as nice as I suspected she would. I have to find her. I didn't train her, didn't fulfill my obligation to one that I brought into the family. Picking up my phone, a few taps has a call going through to my assistant."I need you to find someone for me."

"What is the name? Do you have a picture?"

"The name is Olivia Craig. You can find her picture in the back of her books. I need to know where she is living currently."

"Sir, at the risk of overstepping, you know this could be construed as stalker behavior?"

"I understand your concern, but I need to find her. I turned her the night of the party."

"The party?"

"The party. I turned her on the way to it. I had planned to pick her up the next night. As you know, I was unavoidably detained that night and, much as it shames me, I forgot about her. She was nearly dead when I found her curled up around that stupid dog. She has had none of the required training. At this point, she is a liability."

"I'll get right on it, sir. According to her website, she is in Scotland. I'll get your flight booked and I'll have her address before you get to the airport."

"Thank you."

Twenty-Two

D uncan

Two days is an eternity when I know she is with the shifter. Every time he leaves his house, he looks at the house I'm in, like he can see me, and grins. The sonofabitch grins. She has been taking the dogs out back for two days. I can't even sneak around and be able to watch her covertly there without causing an incident. When she emerges from the house tonight, it's all I can do to keep from running over there. I count to fifty as slowly as I can before I exit the house and walk slowly over there. As I draw near, I realize I should have counted longer. The shifter has his tongue down her throat and her legs are wrapped around his waist. I hate him so much. All I want to do is rip her away from him, but I know that is the fastest way to lose any chance I might have with her in the future. Instead, I walk up behind her and say, "You did promise Roman that you would be back tonight. He is waiting."

The shifter growls as he breaks the kiss, "Go away, vampire."

Olivia shifts and puts her legs down. They aren't touching the ground yet, but she tells Blair, "Set me down."

He kisses her more, loud kisses punctuating every word. "But. I. Like. You. Up. On. Me."

I make retching noises as she laughs and makes him put her down. His raised brow entertains me. She tugs him down and whispers something in his ear and his eye drift closed as a satisfied smile grows on his face. I would love to wipe that smile off his face. "Olivia, are you ready to go home?" Ah, that worked. She kisses his forehead and then his mouth as she tells him she'll see him soon. Once they move away from the passenger side, I get in and watch as he opens her door, and she lets him. Once the door is closed and she is talking out the window to him, I interrupt. "Do you have your dress ready for tomorrow night?"

They both stop and look at me. Olivia says, "What dress? What is tomorrow night?"

"It must have slipped my mind with all that has happened and not seeing you for two nights. Tomorrow is the vampire ball. All of the local vampires will be there. Including any that happen to be in the area. It's a grand affair. I don't understand how you have missed it all these years."

She shrugs, saying, "I would be ok with staying in my room and missing it this year too."

"Sorry, you are being adopted into the family. You are

going to be required to attend them any time you are in the area."

"Great. I will start looking at real estate elsewhere. Blair, I guess I need to go. Apparently, I have to find a dress for tonight."

He kisses her forehead. "Go talk to the witches. They'll get you set up and you can make Duncan wait in the car with the dogs while you and Nims go in."

Twenty-Three

Callum

The last time I went to a ball, it took me several months to recover. I have been loathe to attend one ever since. I must tonight if I want any chance of finding my little Olivia. She hasn't been at her home in days. No one will speak of her here and they become very suspicious about people asking where to find her. Everyone in an area is supposed to go to these things. Surely she will be at this one.

The hotel concierge knocks. He must have my suit back and ready. Once I have collected it from him, I get showered and changed. I think, perhaps, I will go out to dinner before I head for the ball. They always serve bullshit finger food and blooded wine with precious little blood in it at these things.

As I am walking to the restaurant, I see her. Driving by with a man in the vehicle. They seem to be arguing. That's fine. When she goes back home with me, to her family, there will be no more arguments with him. I can save her from his nonsense. She'll be grateful to finally have the mentor and family she should have had from the beginning. If only I had stayed with her that day...

I find myself excited at the prospect of seeing her again. I can't recall the last time I was excited about a person who I wasn't going to murder. Even the ones I planned to murder. That was more about getting revenge than any genuine excitement. And revenge was so sweet. The looks of terror on their faces as I flayed the skin from their bodies. The taste of fear in their blood... I lick the point of my fang, puncturing my tongue just enough to feel that delicious pain. I fucking love it.

I need to get myself to that ball. Paying for my dinner takes very little time, but it seems like forever. The need to get to her has been burning inside me ever since I saw her picture on the back of her book. She is even more magnificent than she seemed that night in the park. Those green eyes are bewitching and the little half smile that tells me she has kept all the pain she's ever received. I just want to unleash it and see what kind of hell she would create. Mother is going to adore her once she comes into her own, if the darkness in her books is any indication of what she is hiding.

Getting to the Principal's home is simple here. It is a monstrosity that Roman has lived in for centuries at this point. He keeps it exactly the same as it was when he acquired it. Did he build it? Maybe, it doesn't matter. The enforcer at the door looks me up and down. "What family?"

"Mezzasalma."

He chuckles, "Enter and be welcomed half cadaver family representative."

Ignoring his joke about the meaning of our family name, I enter the house and start searching for her. I want to watch her a bit before she knows I am here. After making a circuit and picking up a glass of blooded wine from a passing server, I know she isn't here yet. A short fanfare announces Roman at the top of the stairs. Pretentious asshole. I turn to watch as it is expected and there she is, on Roman's arm with enforcers trailing behind them. What the hell is he doing with my Olivia? A killing rage rises in me. I push it down with the reminder that they don't know she is mine. She may not even remember me. His hands on her and the enforcer behind her looking jealous is not helping. Moving to the front of the crowd, I stand in the open where she can see me. I see her eyes move over the crowd. Not a trace of recognition in her eyes. Maybe I can excuse this then.

* * *

Olivia

I hate this. Roman came to my room before the ball to let me know that not only would he be announcing my adoption into the family, I would be required to enter with him and be part of the spectacle of his entrance. As I look out at the people gathered before us, I am amazed at how many vampires are here in Inverness. There must be a few hundred people here. I did not know that Roman had already filed the papers to adopt me. I thought he was just saying that. Now I need to find out what I am going to be required to do. He is introducing me. Time to do the pretty twirl we practiced and hope I don't fall on my face. Roman gives me a small nod of approval as I return to my place beside him.

"Now that you have met our Olivia, I am happy to announce that we are adopting her into our family. She will be one of the Sluagdach, now Slora. Our family expands with one brave enough to face the change to our kind, alone and unknowing. She has faced every challenge with bravery and intelligence, we are honored to have her as one of our own."

Everyone cheers and, as Roman said would happen, people line up to congratulate us. After the first twenty or so, they all seem the same. People kiss my hand over and over like I am some sort of royalty. It's ridiculous. I just wish this could be over. That I could be upstairs with Nims and my dogs instead of Liam and Lauren. I'm not even focused on all the people anymore until I feel the rage. There is a blond man a couple of people back that is angry. So angry I am a little concerned. I know Roman and the enforcers see him too when Roman tugs me closer to his side at the same time as they move to stand a little forward of us. The man smirks like he realizes we have noticed the threat in his anger and it amuses him. The people ahead of him move through too fast and then he is before us.

"Hello, Olivia. It's been a very long time since I saw you."

"Do I know you?" The enforcers have dropped all pretense of ease, surrounding the man. He is still completely relaxed for all his rage.

He smiles and I watch him lick one fang, slicing his

tongue and savoring it. "You do know me, Olivia, even if you don't remember me, and you don't, do you?"

"No, I do not. I begin to think that perhaps age addles vampire brains. How would I know you?"

"I suppose I have only that fateful party to blame. I was unable to keep my promise and come to find you the next night, like I promised."

Realization dawns on me. It's him! "You! You're the one that turned me!"

Roman grabs my hand. "Let's take this conversation to my study. I am interested to know why a Mezzasalma is here ten years too late to claim one that he turned without consent."

Duncan moves to stand between me and my sire. "Will you come along without a fuss, or will we dance?"

The man laughs. "I'm sure we will dance one day soon, Duncan. Alas, tonight I am more concerned with my darling Olivia, left to her own devices all this time."

Duncan nods, and Roman tugs at my hand. I follow him to his study; keenly aware of the group of enforcers behind us escorting my sire to the study. Roman insists I sit almost even with him and to the right. Duncan and the enforcers exchange looks at where Roman has placed me. I'm a little confused by it, but a lot more interested in the guy that sent Nims and me into being vampires without so much as a clue what was happening.

The man is seated across from us. Drinks are brought in and placed on the low table between us. Once the waitstaff have left, Roman clears his throat. "What made you show up here and announce this publicly today?"

"Ah, yes. Timing. It is especially good for me to have

come forward now, before you can adopt my protégé right out of my family. She deserves the opportunity to have the training she has not had to date and, more importantly, the time to get to know her family. To answer your question, the reason for today is simply coincidence."

Roman leans back, crossing one leg to rest an ankle on the opposite knee. "Do you plan to contest the adoption?"

"I do. She is mine."

Duncan looks as though he might burst. Roman nods. "I see. Then I am afraid I must ask you to leave my home."

The man stands. "How dare you? I am the heir to the Mezzasalma. Being in this region gives me every right to be at the ball."

Roman stands and I stand with him, fuck I hope that's the right thing to do."Those courtesies are revoked when you are up for trial."

"Trial? What trial?"

"Ah, Callum. Ever the hothead, forgetting to look at all the angles. What are the penalties for lack of consent in turning a person? For abandoning a protégé? Did you think you would walk in here, claim to be her sire, and only have to fight the adoption?" He chuckles at the tiniest move-ment of Callum's mouth. "We will have the charges leveled against you made part of the adoption. The only remaining question is, will you leave of your own free will or do my enforcers get to play?"

Duncan grins, saying, "Say you want to play."

Callum smiles at him, licking that tooth again. "Let's."

Before they can move, a crack of thunder rolls through the room. Ailsa and three other witches appear in a blinding flash. "It is truly disappointing that you can't behave better, Callum."

His eyes went round. "Ailsa, what are you doing here?"

Her eyes narrow, "Protecting my interests. You will not fight about this. Sue each other in your courts. Do not lay one finger on each other. We forbid it."

Callum gapes and Roman scowls as he says, "Why are you here in my home attempting to order us? This is vampire business. Go home Ailsa."

She laughs and waves a hand, immobilizing every vampire in the room but me. I can feel that she didn't cast it on me. Why? Probably because I'm not a threat.

Ailsa waits for them to realize they can't move before she speaks. "I am here to protect Olivia. She is my interest. The actions you take today will harm the future and I can't allow that. I will have the word of both familial heads that there will be no violence between your families. Or I can leave you frozen until you feel more agreeable. Roman, I meant what I said before. I will wipe vampires off the face of the earth before I will allow you all to fuck this up. I don't care about your pretentious airs or how very important you think you are. You all will not so much as stomp each other's toes. Are we clear?"

Roman nods. "I have to know. What the hell is so important about her?"

Callum is listening intently as Ailsa says, "Everything. I am watching her always. I don't care what family she is allied with at the moment. Both families will be necessary. Learn to get along now. Does everyone understand?"

Roman nods. "I agree on behalf of the Slora. We will

not attack the Mezzasalma and will only ever defend ourselves should they attack."

Callum bites his lip till he bleeds. "I agree to the same terms on behalf of the Mezzasalma family."

I feel the magic flow through the room as she releases them. I look at her and she winks at me. "Olivia, come see me soon. I miss seeing you in the market. Roman, I'll see you soon. Callum, leave. And come to my store."

He looks her up and down. "You could just pop me over with your magic."

"I could, but I'm old. What if I have an accident and scatter your parts?"

Callum rubs his jaw while Roman suddenly finds something outside incredibly interesting. "I suppose that's a fair point. May I spend a short time with my protégé before I leave? I have questions for her and I am certain she has questions for me."

Ailsa eyes him. "You have fifteen minutes. Every minute after that will become increasingly uncomfortable for you." She claps her hands and I feel the power rolling through the room as all the witches disappear in another blinding flash.

Why do I feel that? It's magic. I've never felt that before. Right? Maybe I am slowly losing my mind with all that is going on. Duncan's eyes meet mine and, as much as he terrifies me with what he wants, I feel a warmth inside. A yearning to be near him that I shove down into the depths where it belongs. I can't trust him. And with the complication to the adoption... ugh. What happens if I have to go with this Callum? I mean, he is gorgeous with the beach boy in a suit look, but obviously intensely fucked up if his visible pain fetish is any sign. Roman turns to me. "If you need anything, Duncan will be outside itching to be in here. Any noise will do."

I can't help but chuckle as they all leave Callum and me alone in the study. "Why don't we sit?"

He smirks at me like he knows I am nervous. "Don't worry, Olivia, I will not hurt you. I must apologize for not returning the next night. I was... unavoidably detained."

"Why did you turn me?"

He looks toward the window as if he could see out. "I don't know. I knew the laws. They are quite specific. Yet, as I passed by and smelled the scent of your blood on the air, I was drawn in. Even covered in dirt and blood, you were achingly lovely. I couldn't resist you. So I initiated the change by feeding you my blood."

"Oh. But why did you leave me alone? I was so scared. Until then, the most rebellious thing I had ever done was move out and stop attending the church."

He chuckles, saying, "I see you have moved well past that, judging by your books."

"You read my books?"

"I did. It was your photo on one of them that drew out the memory of you. The night I turned you, I was on my way to a vampire ball in that region. While there, I was attacked so viciously that it was months before I was fully healed. After, well, I was preoccupied with hunting down my attackers and... possibly that will be too much detail for you."

"I see. I am glad you healed and took care of the problem, as it were. Why are you here now? Why would you want to take me from the community that is a large part of my life now?"

"Because I never intended to leave you to fend for yourself. You have a family. You don't need to be adopted into this one."

"What if I like this family?"

"You already have one. You should at least meet them before you cast them aside like so much trash. In fact, I am going to insist that you meet your family before any decisions are made."

"Why? What makes you think I am not perfectly capable of making my own decisions without your interference? My god, you are so fucking full of yourself. I'm not going anywhere with you. I don't care that you were unable to teach me or introduce me to your family. None of that matters. I still want nothing to do with you!" And there is only a little lie in there. But no one needs to know that my hormones are out of control.

He shifts uncomfortably in his seat. "That is a shame. You will come to meet the family and I will remain a part of your life as your sire."

He shifts again, his lips pressed into a thin line. "What is wrong? Are you okay?"

He shrugs, a lift and drop of one shoulder. "The time allotted to me for our conversation is up."

"Oh, my god!" Jumping to my feet, I run over and tug him to his feet, pulling him toward the door. "Out with you! I will not keep you here talking while you are in pain." The door opens as I say that, Duncan giving Callum a hard look.

Callum allows me to pull him toward the door but tells me, "I want to see you again tomorrow. May I come by?"

"You just don't quit, do you?"

"I am very determined once I know what I want."

"I don't think you should come here again." He stumbles as we get near the door. "I am going to see Ailsa tomorrow night. I'll see you then. Don't antagonize my guards." We reach the front door and the enforcer there opens it for Callum.

"Very well, I will play nice with them. Ailsa will appreciate my obedience." Before he steps out the door, he takes my face in his hands and kisses my forehead. It tingles as I watch him stroll down the driveway.

* * *

Author's Note:

Thank you for reading! If you enjoyed this book, you might like some of my other books, which I have linked on the next page. If you love early access, you definitely want to have a look at my Ream subscription where I release all my writing pretty much as it happens. Email signups get all the news and pictures of my pound puppies. (Does anyone else remember the animated series?)

Olivia's Prison will be going up for preorder very soon, right along with the first book in the other series I am working on, A Dream of Blood. In the meantime, happy reading and sign up for the emails. I promise, I will never sell your info (ew) and I don't email bunches either.

Rhiannon

About the Author

Rhiannon writes steamy paranormal romance. She is an avid reader of many authors in a variety of genre though she tends more toward paranormal.

She has three former pound puppies that she dotes on and three daughters that she adores.

Rhiannon has lived in multiple states though she is currently residing in North Carolina. Wandering, witching, and reading with her puppies and husband are what she does when she isn't writing.

To learn about what is happening in Rhiannon's world and get loads of pupper cuteness, sign up for the by using the QR code below to visit my website.

Also by Rhiannon Futch

Get early access to whatever I am writing now by subscribing

at Ream Stories

The Daughter of the Moon series-

Selena Rose, Daughter of the Moon Book 1

Thorns of the Rose, Daughter of the Moon Book 2

Heart of the Rose, Daughter of the Moon Book 3

The Fate's Chronicles series

A Vampire's Fate

A Vampire's Treasure

A Vampire's Dream

A Vampire's Chase

A Vampire's Fight

Fated for Halloween - only available via email signup

The Belancore Witches of North Carolina series

Witchy Ever After

A Witchy New Year

My Witchy Valentine

Sin series

Sin on a Dark Knight

Sin on a Broken Heart

<u>Sin on a Burning Heart</u>

Sin on a Vengeful Heart

The Vampire Kings Series

Mercy of the Vampire King

Shame of the Vampire King

Pursuit of the Vampire King

Prey of the Vampire King

Reign of the Vampire King

Coming soon!

Love and Vampires Series

Olivia's Fall

Olivia's Prison

Olivia's Flight

Olivia's Family

Warriors of the Old Gods series

A Dream of Blood

A Dream of Wolves

A Dream of Stone

A Dream of Ravens

A Dream of Bones